THE CASE OF THE WRONG WORD

MARILYN SMITH PORTER

Marilyn Smith Porter
MarilynSPorter1217@gmail.com
Paperback ISBN: 979-8-9929138-4-2
Editor: Rachael Horn
Cover Designed By: Victoria Lauren Bryan

TABLE OF CONTENTS

THE CASE OF THE WRONG WORD

The Meaning of the Word 'Opaque' Is Unclear

The New York City Detective squirmed inside of his rented tuxedo. He wanted to scratch an itch but now was not the proper time. He was being addressed by a nice elderly man with a smile that might have been as fake as the bird's nest on the top of his head, but Nick Tracy felt the need to be polite. After all, weddings were supposed to be nice social affairs, and wedding guests needed to be cordial.

And so, squirm he must, as the man with the toupee continued. "… And you just have to meet my wife, Detective. You must have heard of her from the Broadway stage. It's been a few years since she stood before those famous footlights, but in her day, she was quite an actress. Never made it to the leading roles—Bette Davis, Mary Martin, Ethel Merman —they were the big ones at the time. But she could hold her own with supporting roles."

Tracy nodded politely and squirmed some more. "I'm sure my date would love to meet her, Mr. Merrick. She is a big Broadway fan. She tells me she has this collection of playbills from every play she has ever been to. I'll bet your wife's name is in quite a few of them. Why don't I go and get Jennifer? I will meet you back at the bar in five."

With that, Tracy excused himself from the clutches of Mr. Jackson Merrick and went to find Jennifer Parker, his date for the evening. It didn't take much searching; in Tracy's estimation, she was the most beautiful woman in the room with her long dark hair and light eyes. He eased next to her side and whispered in her ear. His request was met with a steady glance as if to say, "Is this really necessary?" but the young woman proceeded to extract herself from the gentleman's never-ending story and backed slowly into Tracy's arms.

"What is this? I'm meeting some old Broadway star? Unless it's Carol Channing…"

"I don't think it's Miss Channing, but he did say that his wife was on the stage back in the '50s. I don't know, maybe she's a nobody. But I thought you might like to make small talk. After all, you were in the business at one time."

Jennifer planted a kiss on Tracy's lips and followed beside him. But as they approached the older couple standing a few yards away, she stopped. Tracy felt her reluctance as she began tugging on his sleeve. "Oh, no, Nick. Do you know who that woman is? I can't…"

Tracy backed up, trying to shield them from the older couple's sight, but it was too late. The man began waving. Soon, the two would be within earshot. Tracy had to talk fast. "What is it? What's wrong?"

Jennifer looked up, her blue eyes filled with desperation. "That's Linda Merrick. I worked with her a few years back, in the early '70s. She got me fired. Said she didn't like my designs. Then she got me blackballed with a couple of the directors. She almost cost me everything."

Tracy started to ease away, but as he suspected, Jackson Merrick was advancing forward, bringing his wife with him. There was no escape. He could feel Jennifer cringe as Jackson bellowed loudly.

"Well, here we are. My dear, this is Nicholas Tracy of the New York Police Department. He is the number one detective in the homicide division. I know his Chief Patton, who tells me that Nick here has quite a reputation. A real star. And not only does he solve murders, but it seems his fellow detectives have dubbed him the Rock Hudson of the NYPD. I believe you can see why. And this beautiful young lady by his side must be his date."

Jackson Merrick turned his body so he was facing the woman to his left. He grabbed for her elbow. "Kids, this is my wife, Linda Merrick. Star of the stage and quite a little actress in her time."

Tracy eyed the socialite actress. *What in a '60s' fever dream was this?* Linda Merrick was decked out in a gown that must have been rescued from Edith Head's film storage. Her neck was draped with over-the-top jewelry, and her ear lobes sagged under the weight of costume chandeliers. Her bleached hair was piled on top of her head in a hairdo reminiscent of the Hollywood heyday of the late '50s or early '60s. Barbara Stanwyck came to mind. Everything about the woman screamed "fashionably overdone." Tracy shook Linda Merrick's milky-white hand with the seven rings. "Nice to meet you, Miss Merrick. And this is Jennifer Parker."

If Linda Merrick's memory was jogged by meeting Jennifer Parker, she didn't show it. Her face was cordial, and her eyes crinkled into crow's feet as she smiled and moved her well-manicured hand from Tracy to his date. But, then again, she was an actress. "Hello, Jennifer. Is that with two 'n's'? And Nicholas. So nice to meet both of you. Oh, to be young again. Jackson and I were once young, like the two of you and, of course, the bride and groom over there. Although I don't believe this union will make it to Christmas, it's a mismatch if I've ever seen one. Anyway, time has had its way with Jackson and me, and now we are just the old couple who is guaranteed to leave the party first. You know what they say, there are two kinds of people at parties - those who want to go home early and those who don't. Unfortunately, most of the time, they are married to each other."

Linda Merrick wheeled around to glower playfully at her husband, then turned the other way to wave her hand in the air as if everyone in the room were following her every move. Before leaving their company, she offered a few parting words to Tracy and his date. "Please don't let us keep you kids from the party. Enjoy yourselves before time has its way with you."

And with that, the ex-Broadway thespian moved effortlessly across the floor with her husband in his one-size-too-small tux, following closely on her tail like a trained penguin. Jennifer scoffed at the retreating pair. "What a lousy performance that was. She was as clear as opaque glass. If she didn't have all that money from her first husband, who bankrolled her career, the closest she would have gotten to Broadway would be waiting on tables in the Times Square Deli."

"Wow, Jen. You really do have a burr under your saddle for this woman. Maybe Linda Merrick has mellowed over time. Should you give her the benefit of the doubt?"

"Maybe. But not without some sort of proof. And I doubt I will get that any time soon because I never want to see her again. So, let's go back to the reception and follow her advice and enjoy ourselves. Maybe grab a couple of glasses of champagne. Weddings are supposed to be happy occasions, and like I said, maybe we will never cross paths with those two again."

Unfortunately, *never* was never going to happen. The wheels of fate were already in motion, as Jen and Nick were about to find out—in a big way.

* * *

A Brain Transplant? No, Thank You. I've Changed My Mind

Tracy would say later that the afternoon began like any other afternoon you would expect after a late-night party: sort of quiet and uneventful. There were vows of sobriety to be considered and then abandoned. Hangover remedies to be attempted no matter how ludicrous. And a complete afternoon of peace and quiet watching some major league baseball game played somewhere and viewed by millions of homebound males throughout the country.

Tracy was stretched out on his battered sofa in his old ragbag sweatpants and NYU tee shirt. He hadn't shaved or showered or even made an attempt to make himself presentable. The perfect way to spend the afternoon. His date from the night before, whom he had persuaded to stay when it was clear that dawn wasn't far off, was in the kitchen making sandwiches and hot chocolate. He could hear her rattling pans and opening and closing the refrigerator. The sound of bliss.

Unfortunately for them both, the telephone on the kitchen counter rang. Tracy yelled out, "Don't answer that," but it was too late. *Teen years are the last time you are happy to hear the phone's for you.* With the end of the ring came the end of the peaceful and idyllic afternoon. Moments later, Jen was standing in the living room doorway, her face a mask of bewilderment.

"Nick, that was Linda Merrick on the phone. I don't know how she got your number. You are not going to believe this; she wants to know if you will come over to her house. Someone has shot her husband, and she needs help."

It was a moment before Tracy could connect the name. Linda Merrick? Linda Merrick? Oh, of course, the wedding reception and the man with the bird's nest toupee and the one-time Broadway actress that Jen hated.

"How did she know I was a cop? Oh wait, I think I told the husband."

"Maybe she inquired about us before she left the wedding. The O'Keefe's are the only ones she would have known to ask. Maybe she called them this morning to get your number here."

"What do you want me to do, Jen? We are not under any obligation to accommodate this woman just because she called. The cops in her precinct can handle this."

"I don't know, Nick. I felt kind of sorry for her on the phone. She sounded desperate and scared. Before this very moment, I don't think I could have imagined Linda Merrick crying, but she was really upset. Maybe you should go."

With serious reluctance, Tracy slid off the comfy sofa and went to get his jacket. This meant no shave and no shower for now. Linda Merrick, star of the Broadway stage, would have to take him *as is*. Tracy scooped up his car keys, gave Jen a kiss on the cheek along with cab fare, and then grabbed for the paper with the Merrick home address. Damn. He must need to have his head examined - maybe a brain transplant - because that Yankee game was going to be a good one.

* * *

A Book about Anti-gravity? You Can't Put It Down

There were already two squad cars parked in front and a patrolman guarding the front door. A bevy of curious bystanders lined the sidewalks behind the yellow crime tape like they were waiting for the Macy's parade. Tracy flashed his badge at the patrolman, who lifted the tape and opened the front door without so much as a nod. He was probably as mad as Tracy to be working on Sunday. There was an earpiece in the cop's left ear. Probably the game.

Once inside, Tracy spoke with the investigating team. Mr. Jackson Merrick had been dead on the living room floor when they had arrived. A single gunshot to the head. Tracy listened to the team and made a note of the pertinent details. Several minutes later, he encountered the Merrick housekeeper, a Mrs. Henderson. She had dark hair pulled back into a knot and spoke with a thick South American accent. Brazilian. Tracy recognized the dialect. From what Tracy could see in the dark hallway, she appeared to be somewhere past the late throes of middle age, with the usual crow's feet and the extra few pounds around the middle. Her hair was graying at the temples.

"I will go and let my missus know that you are here, Detective. She is quite upset. She just sits in that dark room, crying. This is not good, no?"

"No, it's not. And before you go, Mrs. Henderson, maybe you can tell me what happened here."

"It was horrible. I am the one who let this bad man in. He asked for Mr. Merrick - called him by name. I didn't know. I showed him into the living room and went to get the mister, who seemed to recognize the man because he went into the living room and closed the door. It was about ten minutes later that I heard shouting, two men's voices, and then the gun. The Missus came running down the stairs, and we both tried the living room doors, but they were locked tight. And no one answered when we knocked and knocked. So, the missus and I went around to the back of the house and found the terrace doors wide open. We went in, and there was Mr. Merrick lying on the floor."

"And you didn't see anyone leave the house?"

"No. I have only been working here a short time, and I don't know the back of the house and the garden. But I think that whoever that man was, he must have jumped the back fence to escape because no one left by the front door. No, no, no. Not while I was here."

"What did the man look like, Mrs. Henderson? Can you describe him — height, weight, coloring?"

"I guess he was tall. He had a very good posture and stood very straight. He had sort of reddish-blonde hair and light eyes. Oh, and I remember now, he had a large mole on his cheek. Maybe it was a birthmark. I try not to stare. All I know is that it was there."

"Okay. If you remember anything else distinctive about the man, maybe he had an accent or a limp or something like that, call me at this number on my card. And now, just one more question. Can you tell me why it's so dark in the foyer?"

The housekeeper paused and pointed to the overhead lights, some of which were burned out. "I don't know why, Detective, but they have the lights on these - what you call - dimmer things. I think maybe because the Missus... she maybe doesn't like the bright lights revealing too much, yes?"

Tracy nodded as if he knew exactly what she meant. "And now, Mrs. Henderson, please let Mrs. Merrick know that I am here."

The housekeeper smiled and nodded before speaking. "I will see if the Mrs. is ready to receive you, Detective." With one backward glance, Mrs. Henderson scurried away in a flurry. Her dark gray uniform and white apron swayed back and forth as she ascended the stairs to the second-floor landing and then disappeared.

* * *

Tracy was in the living room speaking with the local precinct boys when a patrolman made an appearance and told him that Mrs. Merrick said she was ready to see him. Tracy followed the patrolman upstairs to the sitting room. Once there, Tracy recognized the woman he had met only hours before stretched out on a chaise in the dark, her eyes rimmed red and a delicate handkerchief held to her nose. From what little he could see, the woman was no longer in her party makeup and was wearing a long red housedress that was spread over her legs and made a swishing sound when she moved like it was made of silk. Tracy suddenly couldn't imagine Linda Merrick in anything but the height of fashion. Of course, fashion was made to be unfashionable in twelve months, so to keep pace must be a job in itself.

And Linda Merrick obviously took her job quite seriously. Always the Babs Stanwyck. "Thank you so much, Nicholas, for coming over. As you can see, the police arrived before you. One of the neighbors called in to report gunshots. I would be happy to relate the events as they occurred if you would sit in the chair there. I've told Mrs. Henderson to go lie down. She is quite upset by all of this. She feels as if it were her fault. You know how these Brazilian women can be - quite dramatic and all."

Linda Merrick turned her head and then suddenly broke into a hazy fit of tears; maybe some were real, maybe not. *So, who's being dramatic now, Linda?* "I'm sorry, Nicholas. I hope you don't mind that we met here in the sitting room. Mrs. Henderson has big ears. She has only been in my employment for a short time, so I'm not sure I trust her."

"Can you tell me what happened?"

"I was upstairs when Mrs. Henderson showed the man into the living room. She then told Jackson a man was here to see him. Then, about fifteen minutes later, there was a gunshot. I came running downstairs and tried to get into the room, but the door was closed and locked from the inside. So, Mrs. Henderson and I went around back to the terrace door, which was standing wide open. And inside on the floor was Jackson. He was bleeding from a head wound. And the wall safe was open and empty."

"Lieutenant Roberts informs me that you did not find the gun your husband was shot with?"

"I opened the desk drawer where he kept his gun and saw it was gone. I am assuming that is what the killer used. Do you think he took it with him? If that's the case, I can give you the serial number."

Linda Merrick walked across the room until she stopped at a small desk in one corner. She reached inside the drawer and removed a registration form for a handgun. The serial number was clearly visible in the upper corner. She left the paper on the desktop and returned to her chaise. "Do whatever you have to do, Nicholas. I need help. I want to find out who killed my husband, and I want him apprehended. I will never feel safe in this house if he is out there somewhere."

Tracy looked around. The lead detective, Lt. Roberts, was coming through the door unannounced. He was a rough, burly cop who didn't mince words. He spoke as if Tracy were the only person in the room. "Can I see you, Detective? Now? In the living room?"

"I will be right there," Tracy said in response. He would impart the information on the gun. But he could do some investigating on his own. He turned back to the woman in the red dressing gown.

"Okay, Mrs. Merrick…"

"Linda, please."

"Okay, Linda. I promise to help you in every way possible. But now you have to promise me something - that you will get some of the stage managers to consider Jennifer's set designs again. She is hard-working and talented. She needs help getting her foot back in the door. And please don't tell her that I asked."

Linda Merrick smiled. "You are very straight to the point, aren't you, Nicholas? I believe this is the moment when I'm expected to say, 'Why, of course I will.' And even though you are a little rough around the edges, and I hate blackmail, I think we have a deal. I have it on good authority that you are the best in your field, the number one detective in Manhattan, and this loss of my husband has come at a terrible time. Of course, like lousy reviews, there is never a convenient time for death."

* * *

Hey, Need an Ark? I Noah Guy

The following day, while plowing through his own caseload, Tracy checked on the progress in the Merrick case. Lt. Roberts said he was busy, but he had one of his men fill Tracy in on the details. The house, specifically the living room, had been dusted for fingerprints, but there was none to be found. The room had been wiped clean. According to Robert's man, it seemed Jackson Merrick had been a Broadway producer before his retirement. The townhouse he and Linda occupied had originally belonged to her first husband, a man by the name of Neil Mason.

She had acquired the home after Mason's passing and a few years before meeting Jackson Merrick. She was married to Mason when she was in her twenties and a fledgling actress just beginning her ascent on the Broadway stage. But once Mason was gone and she married the famous Jackson Merrick, the name had been a plus in the industry. And very convenient. She didn't even need to change the initials on her towels.

Tracy made an attempt to investigate the Merricks's financial situation. But it seemed that most of their shared wealth was a result of the first husband's money and what Linda had accumulated through stocks and bonds. The market had been good to Linda Merrick. *Her financial advisor should be commended,* was Tracy's first thought, *as he could obviously see the future. Advised Noah to build that ark, did he?* So, in Tracy's estimation, Jackson Merrick was killed for something in that safe or his outside personal dealings.

The next order of business was to put the housekeeper's description of the man she let into the living room through the database and hope for a match. Tracy had a definite feeling that this was a hit of some sort. The fact that Jackson Merrick knew the man well enough to close the doors to the room told Tracy that Merrick wasn't afraid or mistrustful. And then there was the empty safe, which spoke volumes. Tracy had obtained a list of the contents of the safe from Linda Merrick, but the list could be incomplete; a wife didn't always know everything her husband held in his safe. In truth, Tracy was more concerned about the description of the man. And since Linda Merrick never actually saw the man, all he had to go on was Mrs. Henderson's word. *Reliable?* Maybe.

* * *

By early afternoon, Tracy had put the word out. He was looking for a killer. He knew he could rely on his fellow detectives, but there was so little. Just as he was about to leave for lunch and grab a sandwich at the deli, the phone on Tracy's desk rang. It was Linda Merrick. And she was hysterical. "Detective, I can't believe this. I am so distraught. Nothing like this has ever happened in my life. I feel as though I am suddenly cursed."

"Tell me what's happened."

"It's Mrs. Henderson. The housekeeper."

"Don't tell me she's dead."

"No. Worse. She is missing. She has run off somewhere. and taken all the good silver and half of my wardrobe with her."

* * *

I Once Had a Fear of Hurdles. But I Got Over It

"Okay, tell me again, Mrs. Merrick. You got Mrs. Henderson from the employment agency that you always use. How many maids have you hired from this agency in the last five years?"

"Probably five. I guess I'm tough. And I'm picky. Years ago I went to work on the stage just to get out of cleaning. And I've always used this agency. They send me reliable, honest women."

Linda Merrick and Tracy were in the kitchen, at the marble counter. Tracy had already searched through Mrs. Henderson's room, looking for any traces of the woman. There were none. He slid off the stool and started to pace.

"I'm going to need the name of the agency."

Linda Merrick got up and went to the side drawer and removed a card and some papers. She handed everything over. "Here's the agency's card and a copy of Rachel Henderson's resume and past references that she brought with her. And a photo. It's a bit fuzzy, but it will have to do. She will probably be wearing some of my clothes if she can squeeze into any of them. The ones she took were forgiving."

"Did you call any of these references and ask how Mrs. Henderson had fared in their employment?"

"No. I never do. I figure that's the employment agency's job. They must send me women who have been thoroughly checked and rechecked. I don't have time to do their job for them. I have my own hurdles to jump over."

"And she had only been with you for a week or so?"
"Yes."
Tracy grabbed his coat. "I'm going to the agency in person. You wait here, just in case Mrs. Henderson shows up. Maybe she had an emergency. Maybe she had to attend to something."

"You are grabbing at straws, Detective. You saw her room. She took everything she owned with her. Except, of course, for that cigarette case you found under her bed. I know you are hoping that your lab is going to pull some prints off to make sure she really is Rachel Henderson."

Tracy glanced at the cigarette case in the plastic bag. He slipped it into his coat pocket. "Yes. And in the meantime, please stay near the phone in case she calls. And I will get back to you after I've spoken with this employment agency." With that, Tracy left the Merrick house and headed his car uptown.

* * *

Don't Know the Meaning of Apocalypse?... Don't Worry. It's Not the End of the World

Tracy sat in the lobby of the Midtown Employment Agency until a Miss Mendes was "available to speak with him." After a few minutes of waiting, a young woman in her mid-thirties with dark hair and a timid expression appeared in the doorway and motioned for him to follow. She led him down a long corridor that ended in her spacious office surrounded by tall windows that looked out over the Manhattan skyline. Apparently, finding employees for rich people was a very lucrative business. Miss Mendes's opening remarks were the "usual" in the police investigation game. "What can I do for you, Detective?"

"I'm here on a missing person investigation."

Miss Mendes's dark brown eyes lit up. "Oh, I thought you were here for a housekeeper. I was just about to ask you—live in or out? Because we have both. I guess that question won't be necessary now."

Tracy shifted his attention to his notebook. "I'm checking into a Mrs. Henderson that you sent to Linda Merrick's home for employment. I believe the woman may have originally been from Brazil. I need to know how well she was screened. Mrs. Merrick never checked her references, and now she has gone missing. And she took some of Mrs. Merrick's possessions with her. I would like to find her."

Miss Mendes looked calm and collected as she pulled her file drawer open and glanced up, peering over the edge of her tortoise-shell glasses. "What was the woman's name again... that we sent to Mrs. Merrick?"

"Rachel Henderson. Here's a photo. It's not too clear."

Miss Mendes glanced at the photo and then began thumbing through her files at a rapid pace. She seemed to pause about halfway through the drawer. She looked up with a pinched face that was quite unattractive. "Give me a moment, Detective."

She then pulled some other papers from a different drawer and scanned them diligently before looking back at Tracy. The look said, "This is not going to end well."

"Are you sure about the name? I remember last week, Mrs. Merrick called and asked us to send over some women for consideration. She had fired the last one, a Miss Walters. She does this quite often. Everything is 'the end of the world' for Ms. Merrick. So, we sent four or five potentials. She called later and said she had decided on one, but I personally never asked which one. That would have been up to our accounting department. They would have been the ones who need to know."

Miss Mendes looked back at her paperwork. She shook her head slightly. "I will check, but I'm staring at the list of prospective women that we sent to Mrs. Merrick's home: a Miss Jones, a Mrs. Lawrence, and a Mrs. Rayburn—none of them were even Brazilian."

"And, you are positive?"

"Yes, sir. I am positive. We do not have anyone in our files named Henderson. I'm sorry I couldn't have been more help, but if you ever need a domestic, please keep us in mind."

* * *

Tracy went back to the Merrick residence on a whim. Maybe he just wanted Linda Merrick to know he was on the job. Or maybe something in the back of his mind was bothering him. The lady of the house answered the door and showed him into the living room. For the first time, she looked less like the "grieving widow" and more like the star of the Broadway stage. She was in full makeup and actually managed a slight smile. "I haven't replaced Mrs. Henderson yet. The agency is sending someone over tomorrow."

Tracy looked around the room as if appraising its contents. "I noticed, Linda, that you haven't touched the room since we left. Even the wall safe is still ajar. Are you thinking…"

"I'm not thinking anything, Detective. I just haven't gotten around to tidying up. And I don't want to close the wall safe, as I do not know the combination. My husband installed the safe when he moved into my home here after the wedding. To house his papers and valuables. I never asked him for the new combination. Silly of me, I know."

Tracy took one last look. "Okay, Linda. I will be in touch with you soon. Don't worry, we are going to find Mrs. Henderson, and we are going to catch this man who killed your husband."

"I know you are, Detective Tracy. I'm counting on it."

* * *

Did You Know They're Not Making Yardsticks Any Longer?

Two days later, Tracy was at his desk shuffling papers when he received a call from Lt. Roberts. The lieutenant had quite a story. In fact, the story was so long and convoluted that he invited Tracy over to his precinct to hear what a woman by the name of Janice Olsen had to say. It involved the Merrick case.

Tracy borrowed a squad car—his car was in for repairs—and drove to the neighboring precinct. He found Lt. Roberts in one of his interrogation rooms with a sweet-looking, middle-aged woman wearing a raincoat and a ten-gallon cowboy hat that would have made any Texan proud. Tracy took a seat across the table from the woman and looked at Lt. Roberts questioningly. The lieutenant turned to Janice Olsen. "If you wouldn't mind repeating your story, Ms. Olsen, for Detective Tracy."

The woman nodded. When she did, the cowboy hat rocked back and forth. "Well, I was in line at my dry cleaners, talking to this woman behind me. Said she was from Brazil. I really wasn't paying much attention. I eventually got my dry cleaning. But when I got home, I found a pawn ticket inside my coat pocket. I have never been to a pawnshop in my life. But my spinster sister passed away recently, and she was always borrowing my coat—we lived together for forty years— I thought it may have been hers. So, I went to the pawnshop, it is only a few blocks from my house, and lo and behold, the item pawned was a gun. I asked the pawnshop clerk what the woman looked like who pawned the gun. He described the woman, but it wasn't my sister. Maybe the clerk was near-sighted like me. Or had a bad memory. You know, you need a yardstick nowadays to measure the worth of someone's memory. Anyway, I brought the gun home and stared at it

17

for a couple of hours and was actually going to give it to my nephew to keep, but that night, my house was broken into, and they took a bunch of stuff, including the gun. I called the police; a really nice young officer came to the house…and then this morning Lt. Roberts here called me to come into the station. And here I am."

Roberts turned to Tracy. "We caught the punk who robbed Mrs. Olsen. Amateur. The boys down in the lab have the gun. But the reason I called you is because the serial number matches the one you gave me that belonged to Jackson Merrick and was probably used to kill him. I know you have a personal interest in the case. Thought you might want to know."

Tracy looked back at Janice Olsen, who had a look of terror on her face. "Ma'am, it's okay. Please don't be alarmed. No one suspects you of murdering anyone. Now, can you give me the details the pawn clerk used to describe the woman who pawned the gun?"

"Yes, Detective. Middle-aged, paunchy, with dark hair graying a bit. Maybe about 5'5''. He said she had a thick Spanish accent. Not Puerto Rican, definitely Spanish."

Tracy cleared his throat and directed his final question to Janice Olsen. "And now, think back if you can and describe the woman you were conversing with in line at the dry cleaners that day. Does that description match with her as well?"

Janice Olsen thought for a brief moment. Her eyes brightened. "Yes, it does, as a matter of fact."

Tracy produced the picture of Mrs. Henderson that Linda Merrick had given him. "Take a look at this photo, Ms. Olsen. It's not very clear, but…"

Janice Olsen didn't need glasses to see what she needed to see. "Yes, Detective. This is the woman behind me in line. I would swear on a stack of Bibles. Only thing different— she was wearing a bright pink dress with a big colorful peacock on the shoulder. Do you think she slipped the ticket in my pocket while we were in line?”

“Yes, I do. I think she pawned the gun, went home and changed, and then found you in the dry cleaner’s shop. She used you. But I don’t think she had a crystal ball. She didn’t see the robbery thing coming.”

The cowboy hat moved with Janice Olsen’s head as she looked from Tracy to Roberts and back again. “Glad I could help. But now, if you gentlemen will excuse me, I have to go home and feed Homer. He doesn’t like his evening meal to be late since we moved here from Oklahoma.”

“Husbands are like that sometimes,” Lt. Roberts offered with a smile.

“Oh no. Homer isn’t my husband, Lieutenant; he’s my dog. Mexican chihuahua. Hairless.”

And with that, Janice Olsen stood and left the interrogation room. She passed the lab boys, who were on their way in. They addressed Roberts, passing off the bagged gun to Tracy for a quick look. “No prints on the gun, Lieutenant, other than Mrs. Olsen’s.”

Lieutenant Roberts turned to Tracy. “I will call you if we get any more leads, Detective. After she pawned the gun and got rid of the ticket, Mrs. Henderson probably took a plane out of the country. Or at least out of the state.”

Tracy didn’t quite agree. “Never say never, Roberts. I think you will agree that there has to be a reason that Mrs. Henderson wanted that gun found. She must have been hoping that Janice Olsen would take the ticket into the pawnshop and get the gun. Otherwise, why not just throw it away? What about the thief you have in custody? Could he be connected to the case? Did someone pay him to rob the house knowing the gun was in there?”

“Not too likely. He is just a small-time crook—done a few stints in prison for petty theft. He has no connections

to any gangs. You can question him if you like. We didn't
find anything to point in the direction of the Merricks."

Tracy stood and made his way to the door. "Thanks.
I'll do that. But your boys are pretty thorough. Doubt if I
will find anything that they didn't." Tracy left the
interrogation and made his way to the front. He didn't want
to step on any toes in his effort to help Linda Merrick, but
he didn't want to leave any loose ends either.

* * *

My Tailor is Good. Or Sew it Seams

Tracy and Jennifer Parker stared at the lavish
dessert at the same time. They turned to their hostess with
anticipation over the first bites. Linda Merrick had
promised that dessert would be a masterpiece. Mrs.
Henderson's replacement had turned out to be a whiz in the
kitchen. According to Linda, the new housekeeper's
strawberry shortcake was "over the moon." Tracy and Jen
were not disappointed. They waited for their hostess to
speak. The wait was short.

"So what you are telling me, Detective, is that Mrs.
Henderson, whom the agency never sent over, pawned
Jackson's gun, and a lady found the ticket and took the gun
home? Is that even possible?"

Tracy nodded before swallowing the bite.
"Yes. And the lady who had the gun was robbed, and when
the thief was apprehended, the gun was still in his
possession. The serial numbers matched perfectly with your
husband's gun. When he was arrested, the thief made a full
confession."

Linda Merrick looked disappointed to find she
hadn't discovered a loophole in the system. "I see. Well, at
least we know now that Mrs. Henderson, or whoever she is,
was part of the murder plot against my husband. She didn't
pull the trigger, but she let someone inside this house who

20

did. She must have been a plant, part of the plan all along. Can you please find her and this mystery man, Detective? I won't feel safe until you do...So, I'm thinking of taking a trip, a vacation, just to get away."

"Detective Roberts from the local precinct is on the case, as you know. Between the two of us we will keep the search alive. Which reminds me, I need a list of the items that Mrs. Henderson took with her. Especially your missing clothes."

Linda Merrick left the room and was back within seconds carrying a list. Tracy glanced over the items. Halfway down the page, there it was: a hot pink sheath with a peacock emblem on the shoulder.

Jen placed her hand on top of Tracy's. She squeezed lightly as she looked to Linda Merrick. "Nick will do everything he can, Linda. And I'm so glad you insisted we stay for dinner tonight. This was a treat. And thank you for recommending me to a few of the stage managers. I received two calls today."

Thirty minutes later, the couple were back on the street heading to Jennifer's apartment. It was a warm night, so they decided to forego a taxi, opting to stroll shoulder to shoulder. Once back in the apartment, Jen left to go make coffee, and Tracy waited in the den. He went to the bookcase and removed the leather-bound book containing Jen's playbill collection. Most had her name listed as a set designer. It was impressive. She had worked on over 20 plays both on and off "the great white way." Some revised productions. Some off-Broadway trials. Tracy flipped through the pamphlets looking for one that contained the name Linda Merrick. He found several. She had quite a diverse career. No big extravagant production musicals like Chicago or South Pacific. Most were serious dramas.

When Jen re-entered the room with the tray of coffee, she seemed amused that Tracy had found the energy to cruise through her collection. "Looking for Linda's credits and quotes?"

"Yes. And I found a few." *Linda Merrick, star of the stage...quote...never forget who you are, because the rest of the world will not...end quote.*

"Oh, and don't forget she used to be Linda Mason, in the early years. Here, I will show you." Jen grabbed for the early books and thumbed through until she happened upon what she had been looking for—the name Linda Mason in bold type. She handed the early books to Tracy, who had a few questions of his own.

"What was she like in the early years?"

"Not much different than she is now. I first met her when I was an apprentice. By the time I moved into head set designer, she was moving up the ranks herself. Sometimes, we would both be working on the same play. One day, we met for coffee after running into each other on the street. She was coming out of the shop of her favorite tailor, Mr. Ferragamo; he is a really good alterations man, by the way. Her husband had recently passed away. I heard the insurance policy was substantial. Then, after our coffee date, she suddenly became dissatisfied with my set designs. Complained to the directors and the playwrights. She got me fired and practically blackballed. And you know the rest."

Tracy nodded, not really paying attention. There was something that had caught his eye—Something interesting. He was comparing today's Linda Merrick with the stills from one of Linda Mason's plays, *Where's Charley?* circa 1957. There was a major difference.

"So, Nick, do you think they will ever catch this Mrs. Henderson and the man who came to the door and shot Jackson Merrick?"

Tracy set aside the playbill and gave his full attention back to his beautiful friend. "It's possible. But I think we know two things for certain: Mrs. Henderson and this unknown man plotted to kill Jackson Merrick. And Mrs. Henderson got rid of the gun at the pawnshop and put the ticket in Janice Olsen's coat pocket. But the real kicker to all of this is the 'why.' Why did they want Jackson Merrick dead? And why did they want the gun to be found?..."

The answer to those questions was going to be a shocker of huge proportions.

* * *

Big Paddle Sale at the Boat Store.
Quite an Oar Deal

Tracy opened the pawnshop door and stepped inside, out of the spring rain. He brushed off his trench coat and approached the front desk. A small man in a turtleneck sweater and a scarf stood on a box behind the counter, awaiting his arrival. *Had he seen Rod Steiger's portrayal of the pawnshop broker? Apparently.* Tracy brought out his badge and showed the little man.

"And how can I be of assistance, Detective? I haven't been robbed lately, so it can't be about that, am I right?"

"Yes, sir, you are. I am inquiring about a lady who pawned a gun here the other day. Another lady in a cowboy hat came in and retrieved the gun— she had the ticket. But I'm most interested in the woman who pawned the gun. I have a photo." Tracy produced the snapshot of Mrs. Henderson. "Is this the woman?"

"Yes, it is. She had a thick Latin accent. She might have referred to Brazil. Called the gun a pistola."

"And you're sure this is the woman?"

"Yes. I must remember my customers, Detective. I run a pawnshop. I even remember…the blouse in this picture is the same as the one she was wearing when she came in. It's her."

When Tracy arrived back at the precinct, everyone was in, even Chief Patton, who was in his typical bad mood. Tracy tip-toed past the chief's office, entered his own, and slid behind his desk piled with papers that needed his attention. But before he dove into the pile, he called the records department and asked to see a death certificate from some years back. They said they would rush it through.

A few hours later, Tracy had what he was looking for. The certificate said that the cause of death was a substance overdose. That meant it could have been an accident, or it could have been a suicide. Interesting. Of course that also meant, once again, he was up the creek without a paddle. So, he put in a call to Lt. Roberts in the neighboring precinct. There was no news on the Merrick case. There were no fingerprints, latent or otherwise, anywhere. All prints were accounted for. And there were no hits on the description of the man who came to the door. It was now assumed that Mrs. Henderson and the man were partners, which was baffling, as Jackson Merrick knew the man and felt comfortable enough to close the door to the living room. So, who was the man?

Of course, Mrs. Henderson's description of the man was now discredited. No doubt meant to throw the police off the track. Forget the large mole and the ramrod posture. Mrs. Henderson's description was absolutely useless.

Tracy threw a dart at his nearby board. And then another. And another. Finally, a bull's eye. And as he leaned back in his chair, staring at the direct hit—it came to him. Just like that.

* * *

I'd Eat a Clock, but It's Quite Time-Consuming

Tracy called Lt. Roberts first thing in the morning. He wanted to know if his men had pulled any fingerprints off Mrs. Henderson's cigarette case. When he was told the only prints on the case were blurred, Tracy was disappointed. He told Roberts he had written a report and was sending it over by messenger. It was an accumulation of all the facts he had gathered. What wasn't in the report was the fact that he was now fairly confident he knew how Jackson Merrick died. But he had no tangible proof. Yet. Any accusations never could've been proven in a court of law.

At lunchtime, Tracy met Jen at a small diner around the corner from her new assignment. She left someone named Ricardo in charge and came to meet Tracy at 12:45. It was a nice leisurely lunch, with both unwilling to cut their time short. Tracy had kept Jen tuned into the Merrick case every step of the way, so there was a bit of catching up to be done.

When they finally forced themselves to return to their respective jobs, Tracy walked Jen back to the theater stage door. They lingered on the sidewalk for a moment, oblivious to the passing pedestrians who were equally unaware of their presence. When Tracy finally left and headed back to the precinct, there was something in the back of his mind. He wasn't sure what it was, maybe nothing, but he needed to find out.

It had to do with Mrs. Henderson. And proof. Perhaps it was closer than a stone's throw away. So, instead of turning right and heading to his car, Tracy turned left and walked a few feet. And there, staring him in the face would be all the proof he needed. What was that old saying? *Truths are worth lying for.* Or was it… *Some truths are best left unsaid.*

25

* * *

Check the Bowl, but I Think
We're Plum out of Fruit

Tracy was sitting in the living room of the beautiful townhome in mid-town Manhattan. And he was staring down the barrel of a loaded gun. Nobody had bothered to ask Linda Merrick if her husband owned more than one gun. Pity. "Linda…"

"That's Mrs. Merrick to you, Detective Tracy. I think we can drop the niceties now."

"Okay, Mrs. Merrick. Look, you don't want to do this."

"Yes, I do. When I call the police, and they find your body, I will tell them Mrs. Henderson and her murderous accomplice did it. They showed up here while I was upstairs packing for my trip. You were waiting downstairs to drive me to the airport. I heard talking. I recognized Mrs. Henderson's voice, and then there was a gunshot. So I hid in my closet."

Linda Merrick held the back of her hand to her damp forehead as if she were about to faint dead away on the carpet. *Method acting.*

"Oh, I am so upset, so traumatized, Officers. Poor me."

Tracy was starting to sweat. Just a little. "What can I say to change your mind, Mrs. Merrick? I've got an apartment full of sweet, helpless animals that depend on me to feed and house them. You wouldn't want to make them orphans, would you?"

"That's a shame, Detective. But when you stepped into that alteration shop today and talked to Tony Ferragamo—he called me after you left by the way…then I knew you were too close to the truth. You know too much. So now you must go, permanently."

"Why would you do this? You have more than enough money. You're beautiful, famous..."

"You can stop with the flattery, Detective. I won't fall for that stuff from you or any other man."

"What can I do?"

The actress smiled for the first time since Tracy had arrived at the house at Linda Merrick's insistence. "Nothing, Detective. It won't do you any good. I've made up my mind. It must be done this way."

Tracy stood and reached into his coat pocket. He didn't give Linda Merrick a moment to consider what he was doing. She had already relieved him of his gun, so she didn't look too worried. He pulled out his badge, all the while moving sideways, positioning himself. "See this badge, Mrs. Merrick? Take a close look because this means something. In fact, a great deal to every cop on the NYPD force."

"I don't care what it means. To me, it means nothing whatsoever."

Tracy was now within arm's length of the wall safe. "We have a code among the guys in blue, Mrs. Merrick. If we are ever in serious trouble and we have to leave a message for those who follow to tell them who the guilty party is, we leave our badge."

"So what, Detective? That doesn't concern me in the least. After I kill you, I will just take that badge and heave it into the Hudson."

"I don't think so." With that, Tracy tossed his badge into the empty safe, whose door was still ajar, and slammed it shut. He turned the dial a few revolutions and then whirled around to face his aggressor. Linda Merrick's face was in shock, and then she was livid.

"Why did you do that, Detective? What in the hell do you hope to gain by such a move?"

"Like I said, we have a code on the force. Every cop knows exactly what a badge left behind means. When they come here and find my body, they will search every nook and cranny in this room, including that lovely little safe one of our locksmiths will open…and they will find my badge inside and know that you are the killer. Then the D.A. will convict you. There is nothing more unforgiving than a cop killer."

"That's preposterous, Detective."

"Is it really, Mrs. Merrick?"

"I will just go open the safe and get the badge out."

"No, you won't. You told me yourself that your husband never told you the new combination. That's why you've left the door open all this time."

"Then I will call a locksmith right now to come open it."

"You won't do that either. You don't have the luxury of time. Everyone at the station knows where I am. I have to log out when visiting someone involved in an open case. Especially a case from another precinct. And I am required to check in every thirty minutes. If I don't, the boys back at headquarters will come and check, and they won't wait any longer than..." Tracy consulted his watch. "Oh, about ten minutes from now is my guess."

Linda Merrick's finger tightened on the trigger of the gun. "I could just leave here right now. What's been said here in this room tonight... well, it's your word against mine. And haven't you heard, Detective? I'm a great actress on the stage. I can be very convincing when I want to be. But if you promise to give me some time, I will leave the country and never come back. I've told everyone I know that I'm taking a trip to deal with the loss of my husband and out of fear of the killers working with our Mrs. Henderson."

Tracy put his hand out to stop the flow of words. "You won't do anything, Mrs. Merrick, other than give me the gun."

Linda Merrick shook her head. "Sorry, Detective, but for once, you are wrong. I'm going to call a cab, and then I'm going to the airport with my packed bags that are sitting out there in the hallway. And you will stay right there and wait to give me a head start. Do we understand each other?... Good. And now you will call the station in my presence so I can hear what you say. Tell them all is well. And then I will walk out that door. And you will be on the clock for five hours. Do we understand each other, Nick?"

Tracy nodded his consent. And then he followed her instructions. He called the station; they were a bit surprised to hear from him. When he hung up the phone, he heard the screech of the tires as the taxi pulled up out front of the house. After Linda Merrick finally left, lugging her suitcases to the waiting cab, that's when Tracy fell to the sofa in a total sweat and tried to slow down his beating heart, which was threatening to jump out of his chest. Only 4 hours and 59 minutes to go.

* * *

Japanese Sword Fighting?
I can Samurais It for You in One Sentence

It was late night. Tracy and Jen were lingering over coffee in a neighborhood café that was nearing closing time. The manager, a nice little man by the name of Bobby Bott, had instructed his crew to work around his customers. So there was no need to rush. And Tracy had a lot to say. "I think I knew it all along, but I couldn't put together exactly how. And forget the "why." I doubt we will ever know. But yesterday, when I left you at the theater, I knew I would find the answer somewhere nearby. And I did."

Jen rolled her eyes with impatience, prompting Tracy to get to the point. "Just tell me how."

"It was actually very simple. As you know, when Jackson Merrick was shot, Linda Merrick called my house and had me come to the residence. When I got there, I spoke with the housekeeper, Mrs. Henderson. Nice lady, but she said she was new. She had already given her statement to the police. She went upstairs to get Linda, and then Linda and I spoke in her upstairs sitting room. Her husband's gun was missing, but she had the serial numbers. A cop's dream. Forty-eight hours later Mrs. Henderson disappears from the Merrick house. No one knows where she went or who she really is because the employment agency did not send her to the Merricks. All we knew was that she was from Brazil. But then she shows up at the pawnshop, pawns the murder weapon, puts the pawn ticket in Janice Olsen's coat at the dry cleaners, and lets human nature take its course. Mrs. Olsen, being curious, gets the gun out of the pawnshop, and with a bit of an unexpected twist, the gun is stolen in a robbery at Janice Olsen's house and then recovered by the police."

"And so, how did you find out who Mrs. Henderson really was?"

"From you."

"Me?"

"Yes. The playbills. Linda Mason, pre-Merrick, had a supporting role in a play called *Where's Charley?* in 1957. She played the part of Donna, Charley's aunt from Brazil. And when I looked at the stills in the playbill, I didn't realize it at the time because they were old and fuzzy and black and white, but I was looking at Mrs. Henderson. A few years younger, but there she was, costume and all. And if I was right, the now older and thinner Linda Merrick would have to have the costume altered to fit her frame. So the other day, when I left you at the theater, I went next door to the little tailor who does all the alterations for the theater people. I read somewhere that most actresses keep their costumes for sentimental reasons. Linda Merrick is no exception. After I flashed my badge, the nice gentleman told me Linda had brought the costume to be taken in. However, the little tailor said the costume was old and fragile. To try and alter it would have been disastrous. So, my guess is that Linda had to wear some padding beneath the costume to make it look right. Which actually worked in her favor."

Tracy accepted a refill from the passing waitress. He thanked her before returning to his story. "At first Linda Merrick made the mistake of wearing the costume out on the street. The pawnshop clerk told me she was wearing the same outfit as in the picture. I thought that was odd. If she was on the lam, she would want to wear something different to disguise herself. Linda Merrick told me that Mrs. Henderson absconded with some of her clothes. Maybe she came to the realization that she had better be seen wearing some of those clothes. So she picked the most distinctive dress. The one with the big peacock on the shoulder. Who could forget that? Certainly not a lady wearing a cowboy hat."

Jen smiled. A big toothy grin. She grabbed for Tracy's hand. "Pretty smart, Detective. But what sealed the deal?"

"I think it was when I realized that Mrs. Henderson and Linda Merrick were never in the same room at the same time. Linda made excuses for Mrs. Henderson that first day I met with her by saying she had the woman go lay down because she was so upset, while she herself was sitting in a dark room, with no makeup and a hankie in front of her face. She must have rushed upstairs removed the wig and the dark makeup that she had needed to make herself into Mrs. Henderson and positioned herself on that chaise. Linda Merrick re-created the role she played years ago. She even adopted the thick Brazilian accent."

"So, who was the man who came to see Jackson Merrick? Someone that Linda Merrick hired to kill her husband?"

"There was no man."

"No man?"

"No. That was just a lie. Linda Merrick had her husband open the safe because she didn't know the combination, after which she proceeded to empty out all the valuables. And then she shot him with his own gun, opened the terrace door, and then came inside to call me. She must have gotten the idea to use us when we met the night before at the wedding reception. When she found out that I was a detective, she may have thought that I was a good patsy to make the whole thing look real."

"But why pawn the gun and put the pawn ticked in the woman's pocket at the dry cleaners?"

"Because she needed someone else to see Mrs. Henderson. To create the illusion that the housekeeper was real. She created Mrs. Henderson to give herself an alibi, and she did that beautifully with me and with the police. But we may have questioned Mrs. Henderson's existence eventually. So she had to have the housekeeper on the run. She probably waited in that dry cleaner until an older woman came in. My guess is that she picked Janice Olsen out as a person who would probably strike up a conversation in a line. A cowboy hat in New York City? And once she spoke with her and heard her sister had recently died, she knew that Ms. Olsen would be naturally curious about the ticket and maybe even turn it into the police. We had the serial number off the gun, thanks to Linda, so she knew we would match up the gun, the stolen dress with the peacock on the shoulder, and Mrs. Henderson. So she slipped the ticket into Janice Olsen's pocket. And Janice took the bait."

"So, there are two people who had verbal contact with Mrs. Henderson: the dry-cleaning lady and the pawn broker. Two people who could describe her and who would remember the thick Brazilian accent and the hot pink dress."

"Yes. But that's where she made her one mistake. When she went to pawn the gun, the clerk told me she referred to it as a pistola, which is Spanish for gun. Despite what everyone believes, Brazilians don't speak Spanish. They speak Portuguese. And the word for gun in Portuguese is arma de fogo, not pistola."

"Nice work, Detective Tracy."

"Thanks. She almost had me. She was clever. She created Mrs. Henderson, and by the time the agency figured out she didn't employ any of their candidates, Jackson would already be dead, and Mrs. Henderson would be on the lam."

"So what turned the great actress Linda Merrick into a killer?"

"I believe she already was one."

Jen shook her head from side to side. "You don't mean…the first husband?"

"Yes. I checked into his death. It could have been poisoning. My guess is that she killed the first husband for the money. And Jackson Merrick, after all these years, may have started asking questions about Neil Mason's death. Maybe he figured it out. Maybe he even found proof. And maybe the night of the wedding reception, when he discovered I was a detective, he made a point of bringing her over to meet me and tell her I was a homicide detective. She would have perceived it as a sort of threat. Like 'look here, I know a detective now, so you had better be good or I'll blow the whistle'."

Tracy leaned back in his chair. He was thinking that there must be a certain satisfaction for Jen to be in on the final thrust of the sword into her nemesis.

"That, Detective Tracy, was a brilliant piece of work. And now we can only hope that the Swiss police cooperate and extradite her back here to stand trial. You know, you have this little trick you do where you open your mouth, and brilliance comes pouring out."

Tracy felt like the rooster who believes the sun rises just to hear him crow. He rarely got compliments. Of course, he didn't tell her about the incident with the loaded gun pointed at his chest. Or the big bluff involving the story about leaving behind your badge for your fellow cops to tell them who the killer is.

Suddenly, Tracy noticed it was five minutes to closing time, and they were the last customers to leave. He signaled for the waitress to bring the final check. He was just about to stand and reach in his back pocket for his wallet when he observed a man coming through the front door of the restaurant. Bobby Bott saw what Tracy saw and was walking across the floor, waving his arms.

"I'm sorry, sir...we are just closing. Please come back another time." But the man seemed to be ignoring the café owner. He was staring at Tracy and Jen and walking towards them at a good clip. The man was on the short side, well-built, and younger than Tracy. He stopped within inches. "Are you Detective Nick Tracy?" the man asked.

Tracy could barely get the words out of his mouth before the man punched him in the face with his fist. A quick straight-arm jab, right on the nose. Tracy fell backward, spilling onto the floor. The unknown man vaulted over the fallen detective and turned for the door.

Jen started yelling for help just as the café owner and a few of the waiters reached their side. Together, they had Tracy back on his feet. When everyone looked up the man was running out the door; only to disappear into the night. The restaurant owner apologized over and over, declaring that their meal was "on the house."

When Tracy was back in his seat at the table, he thanked everyone while using his left hand to work his jaw back and forth. Jen made sure he had survived the incident, and then she too took her seat. "What just happened, Nick? Do you have a new case?"

"Of what?"

Jen appeared to be trying not to laugh. "Very funny, Detective. Some guy just punched you in the nose, and you are cracking jokes. Really? And fighting in a restaurant?"

"I wasn't fighting, he was. I was lying on the ground."

"Did you know him?"

"No, I didn't know him. And I don't think I want to know him. He was tough and brave enough to hit a New York City Detective. That's all I need to know for now."

"Okay then, let's go back to my place, get some ice on that jaw. I have some pain pills left over from my dental surgery. I think you might need a couple."

With that, Jen and Tracy left the restaurant with the owner still apologizing.

It would be only 24 hours before Tracy would find out exactly who the man was—and why he wanted to punch him in the mouth. And the reason would be a good one. One that Detective Nick Tracy would never forget. Soon, the word would be out, the gauntlet would be tossed, and the challenge posted. Nick Tracy… sorry, but… here you go. Game on.

THE ARREST OF MARY TROTTER

PROLOGUE

"No matter how brilliant our idea, others will only be moved if they believe they have already thought of it themselves."—Anonymous

May 1979 — Midday

It was warm and stuffy in the 19th Precinct's interrogation room in the heart of Manhattan. Across the worn metal table was a woman in her mid-fifties, maybe younger. She was attractive, but her demeanor was cold, cheerless—as if she had slid off the wrong side of the bed that morning and discovered she was a "person of interest" in a police case. And funny thing about that... it seems she was.

"So, Detective. What's the deal? We've been sitting here for over an hour. You've asked me everything, and you've seen my rap sheet. You know I've been convicted several times of forgery. Big deal."

"Any conviction is a big deal, Miss Trotter. But
we're not here talking about forgery."

"Oh yeah? Then what *are* we here talking about?
You have me picked up, brought in, I've answered all your
questions... and you've got nothing on me."

"Oh, but I do, Miss Trotter. Let's start with where
you got the money for your fancy new apartment uptown.
And all the fancy new furniture. And I'm guessing there's a
shiny new car parked in a pricey garage somewhere."

"Where does anyone get money, Detective? I work
for it, I put it in the bank, and then I take it out as I need it,
like every other law-abiding citizen."

"I checked your bank account; in fact, all your
deposits and withdrawals for the last 5 years, Miss Trotter.
Other than your paychecks, there were nothing but a few
small entries. And your withdrawals were typical cost of
living items."

The handsome detective consulted the list in his
trusty notebook. "...Groceries, rent, utilities, hairdresser,
manicurist, psychics (he scoffed a bit at this one), and the
occasional trip to some mall."

Before the woman could reply, the door to the
interrogation room opened, and one of the fellow detectives
joined the pair. Mary Trotter eyed the new addition to their
table. "Oh, I get it now. You bring in this guy that picked
me up in the middle of my office meeting and have him
stand there in the back of the room. Really? What is this
good cop/bad cop like some episode of Starsky and Hutch?
I don't think I like this Detective-even if you are good-
looking and red-hot. Okay, so I lied. I saved the money in
my mattress. I did odd jobs and stuff. All legitimate. And
my mother gave me some."

"Then I will need to see the W-2s or 1099s from
these legitimate odd jobs you were paid for. Do you have
those, Miss Trotter? If so, we can go back to your
apartment and take a look right now."

Mary Trotter shook her head in the negative. "No, I don't have them. I lose stuff, Detective. I'm forgetful. Look, what do you want from me? So I keep a lot of cash. A lot of people do that nowadays. Nobody trusts banks anymore. And besides, I didn't do anything. Did someone say something? If so, it's all lies. Like I said, I didn't do anything."

"I think you did, Miss Trotter. I think you did a lot. Did you go to the Skyler Building yesterday?"

Mary Trotter's face turned a faint shade of red, but her eyes never wavered. Suddenly, she started crying hysterically, which turned into a hiccup-laughter a moment later.

"What's wrong, Miss Trotter?"

The hysteria subsided a bit. "What's wrong, Detective? Maybe the fact that you are asking me what's wrong, for starters."

The detective took a deep breath. His patience was wearing thin. And the fan whirring above their heads was starting to annoy the crap out of him. "Can we get back to the questioning, please? Did you go to the Skyler Building yesterday?"

"Do you really want to know, Detective? Then you will have to start listening because, yes, I was at the Skyler Building yesterday. You obviously know I was, or you wouldn't have made me tell you."

"We also know who you visited, Miss Trotter; we saw the sign-in sheet. I was actually wondering why you didn't forge yourself a new I.D. with a nice little name like Mary Smith. But you didn't. You used your real name. And we also know you were there a second time, but you didn't sign in. Am I right?"

"You're doing the talking, Detective."

"I'll ask you one more time..."

"Look, I've had enough of these four walls. If someone said they saw me there a second time they're crazy. They're lying."

"We didn't need anyone to tell us anything, Miss Trotter. I found a piece of paper on his desk. It said 28=17. It was code. At the end of the day, before you got there, he undoubtedly went down to the guard's desk to see what number you were on the sign-in sheet. You were #17. And that's when he saw that there were 27 visitors to the firm that day. He couldn't write your name on the paper; you would have just thrown the paper away. But if you found this, the numbers wouldn't make sense to you. He might have even guessed you would sneak past the guards on that second visit because you knew the code to the elevator. And he was right. The security company only changed the code in the morning. Very clever. But all we really needed, Miss Trotter, was that little piece of paper. 28 = 17. The 28th person in his office was the same as the 17th person."

Detective Nick Tracy stood and nodded to his fellow detective. Then he turned back to the suspect. "…Mary Trotter, you are under arrest for murder. Go with Detective Bell. He will read you your rights."

* * *

"Why do brilliant ideas sometimes involve felonies?"—K. Reichs

One hour before the arrest of Mary Trotter

New York City Detective Nick Tracy was standing in front of the last known address for a woman named Mary Trotter, a small-time forger who had spent some time in prison due to her blatant disregard for the law that says, "Thou shalt not duplicate other people's signatures or produce documents that are fraudulent." Tracy was staring at a large moving truck that contained boxes and furniture belonging to Mary Trotter, according to the landlord who was standing vigilance over the move.

Unfortunately, the owner of the furnishings in the moving van was not at home. Too bad. Tracy would have liked to have a few words with Miss Trotter. So instead, he approached a large man who was carrying a table on his back as if it were a matchstick. The man was six-foot-something (and the *something* was in double digits), and he was built like a brick house. When Tracy flashed his badge, the man dropped the table as if it suddenly burned his fingers. The big man watched Tracy's every move.

"I wonder, sir, if you could tell me something. I am looking for Mary Trotter, and I know from the landlord standing over there that you are moving her furniture to a new location. Could you please tell me where you are delivering the furniture—the new address?"

Without a word, the big man went inside and hauled out a smaller man (Tracy would not have used the word "smaller" to describe the second man if the first man hadn't been a walking mountain). Tracy repeated the request for information as he once again flashed his badge. "Yeah, Detective. I can give you the address for this Trotter woman... it's here on this paper."

Tracy wrote down the new location for Mary Trotter, thanked the two men, and then headed uptown to the new, more impressive locale. Impressive? That was saying the least.

* * *

"I hope there isn't a problem, Detective. Miss Trotter is moving in today. I would hate to think that I rented that beautiful apartment to someone in trouble."

Tracy ignored the implied question. "I just need to take a look at the new apartment, Mr. Jacobs, and ask you a few questions—like how did Miss Trotter pay you for the rent?"

"She paid cash. The security and cleaning deposit, too."

"Everything was done with cash?"

"Yes, sir."

Tracy made a note in his book and then looked up to see the landlord shaking a bit. "Mr. Jacobs, I wonder if you would show me the apartment that Miss Trotter has rented. And please don't be alarmed."

Landlord Jacobs seemed to get over his shakes as he nodded once and then indicated for Tracy to follow in his footsteps. The luxury apartment building had eight floors. Mary Trotter had rented one of only two units on the top floor. The men rode the elevator up to the eighth in silence and then stepped out. The hallway was luxuriously appointed and furnished with fancy tables and gold sconces. It was all quite a surprise, but not as big a surprise as when Tracy passed through the door of apartment 8C and saw the size of the unit and the attached terrace. Plush carpet, full-blown kitchen with top-of-the-line appliances, floor-to-ceiling windows that were the frame for a view of skyscrapers and city lights. Quite a step up from the place Mary Trotter was leaving.

"I don't have to ask how much this apartment rents for, Mr. Jacobs. Can you please tell me how many months Miss Trotter paid for?"

"Yes, Detective. In addition to the security and cleaning deposits, Miss Trotter paid me for two years' rent. Twenty-four months. I was pleasantly surprised."

Tracy wasn't. And he had seen enough.

Back on street level, Tracy thanked the nervous landlord, who asked for assurance one more time that he wasn't renting to a felon, and then Tracy took the steps down. When he did, he passed a furniture store making a delivery. When questioned, the man said they were delivering to a Mary Trotter in 8C. Tracy directed them to the landlord and then took a look inside the truck. The new furniture looked nice and very expensive.

With that, Tracy went to his car and radioed the precinct. His message? "Here is the address for Mary Trotter's workplace. I want to question her. Have Jim Bell pick her up and bring her in—now."

* * *

"It's easier to fool people than to convince them they have been fooled." —M. Twain

A few hours before the arrest of Mary Trotter

Detective Tracy was fiddling with a pair of ivory figurines from the coffee table at the edge of his knees. He was listening to a narrative that was taking nothing short of forever. The woman speaking was a middle-aged widow by the name of Ann Beasley. He had been lucky to find her. All he had was a name and the fact that she lived in Brooklyn on State Street.

Ann was very average. Average height, 5'4"; average weight, about 130; with a very average face: two small eyes, thin lips, and no real structure. But what Ann Beasley lacked in cheekbones, she made up for in the fact that she had something that Tracy needed: information. So Tracy listened, fiddled to keep his mind on business, and waited for a break in the narrative so he could ask a few questions. The break hadn't come yet.

"And I didn't even know that Davis was out, Detective. It's been so long since I have seen him. I think I told you what happened when we broke up. Yeah, I did. I don't like to repeat myself." *Too late.* "So, I don't even know where he is living or where he is working."

"Okay, Miss Beasley. Can you tell me if you left this apartment yesterday? And if so, where did you go?"

"Yes, Detective. I went to the grocery store; I was there for about thirty minutes. Didn't get much. I chatted with one of my favorite cashiers, so I can give you her name and you can stop in and check with her if you need to corroborate my story. She will remember because we talked about her sciatica nerve..."

"I'm sorry to interrupt, Miss Beasley, but can we please get back to my question? Besides the store, where else did you go?"

"Nowhere, Detective. You can check with my super. He saw me come in. He keeps an eye on all of us single girls in the building. Not sure if it's the fatherly side of him or the lecherous side, but what can you do? I think he means well..."

"And you said earlier you and Davis broke up before he was incarcerated?"

"Yes. He was brilliant, you know. A genius. But no one knew. We broke up right before he was convicted. He was seeing some woman by the name of Mary Trotter. And he could never explain to me why he was going over there to her house all the time. Weird, right?"

Mary Trotter? This was a name Tracy hadn't heard before. "Do you have this Mary Trotter's address or phone number?"

"Yes, I do. I don't know why I kept it all these years. Funny how we do things that we can't really explain. I'm like that, Detective. I remember everything, keep everything. It's like an obsession. One time I..."

No, no, no—not again. "The address, Miss Beasley. I'm sorry, but I really need to be going. So if you wouldn't mind getting me that information."

Ann Beasley stood, crossed the room, and rummaged through the drawer of an old desk with a broken leg and a shim. She turned back with a piece of paper, which she handed to Tracy.

"Thank you, Miss Beasley, and now I'm afraid I have a piece of bad news. And then I will see myself out. No, no, please don't bother."

* * *

Before calling on this Mary Trotter, Tracy made a stop. He entered the large, impressive office building with a front desk where you were screened before being allowed to use one of the three elevators directly behind the young guard who sat at a large marble desk. Next to each elevator was a keypad where a code must be entered. And no one was getting that code without putting their name on the sign-in sheet and showing a driver's license or some sort of identification. There was one sheet for each of the ten firms.

Detective Tracy approached the front desk and showed his badge to the young guard, who smelled of cologne he thought masked the other smell... cigarettes. Unfortunately, such was not the case.

"I would like to see the sign-in sheet for the Courier Agency from yesterday."

The young guard nodded and pulled out a sheet from beneath the marble desk. He shoved the paper in front of Tracy and went back to greet a young woman asking for entrance to one of the law firms on the fourth floor.

Tracy scanned the sign-in sheet. He had been in this very spot the day before, but he had not known what he was looking for. This time, he was searching for a name among the twenty-seven entries. Fortunately, the guard at the desk was required to print the name of the person signing in and their form of identification. And there, on LINE 17, was a scrawling, almost indistinguishable signature. And next to the signature, in the guard's neat and tidy handwriting: *Mary Elizabeth Trotter / New York State driver's license.*

44

* * *

"Why is it that uneducated minds always criticize
brilliant minds?" —K. Nelson

Twenty hours before the arrest of Mary Trotter

Tracy was at his desk doing paperwork, contemplating his life when the call came in. There had been a homicide in midtown, over on Broadway. A high-rise office building; ten floors, ten companies with several employees each.

By the time Tracy arrived on the scene, one of his men was already there, a rookie by the name of Adam Peters. Peters was observing the forensic guys setting up to start on their job, gathering evidence and fingerprints. Peters told Tracy it appeared the guy was hit over the head and then stabbed in the back. In all probability, sometime late the night before.

Tracy entered the office to find a man on the floor, his head and jacket bloody and his face buried deep in the shag carpet. The detective walked around the modest office looking for traces of the man's life. But there were no photos on the desk, none of a wife or kids, no candid shots of his dog or his goldfish. Nothing. Next, Tracy very carefully opened a few desk drawers and rummaged around for personal papers or anything to indicate who the man was and what his life was all about. But once again, nothing.

Forensics were still dusting for prints, so Tracy sent Officer Peters to find out the dead man's name. No one had yet arrived for work at The Courier Agency, which didn't open until ten, so Peters took the elevator down to the manager's office to bring him up for identification. Tracy stayed behind to examine the body further, and when he lifted the man's arm using a pencil from one of the drawers, he discovered something gripped tightly in the dead man's hand. It was a crumpled piece of paper with the numbers: 28=17.

Tracy left the C.S.I. team and went down to the guard station. He asked the day guard to see the sign-in sheet. There were 27 visitors who signed in at The Courier Agency the day before. No number twenty-eight. Suddenly, Tracy had a case of déjà vu. Where had he heard the name Courier Agency in the last few days? The name sounded familiar. It would come to him.

Next, he asked to see the night guard, who was still on the premises. The guard informed him that no one got past him. But when Tracy questioned him further, he admitted he went out back for a smoke but insisted there was no way anybody could get upstairs without the code for the elevator, which is changed every morning. In Tracy's estimation, a cigarette takes approximately five minutes to smoke. Topping that with an additional minute for the time back to the front desk, six minutes is enough time for someone to commit murder, then wait on the stairs for the guard's next cigarette break, allowing them to slip out of the building through the back door.

Tracy looked around the busy lobby and then headed back to the elevator, knowing the code he used earlier would work, and took elevator #3 up to the floor where the man lay dead on the carpet. Officer Peters met him in the hallway. "I have the name of the victim, Detective. He was employed here at The Courier Agency as an expert on internal company theft. His name was Davis Runyon."

Detective Nick Tracy felt the breath leave his lungs as his heart dropped from his chest.

* * *

*"Whatever brilliant ideas you have, the opposite
may also be true." —D. Sivers*

One week before the arrest of Mary Trotter

Detective Tracy entered the offices of Oppenheimer, Goldberg, and Gibbons. In his right hand was an attaché case. After checking in with the girl at the front desk, he took a seat in the waiting room and read a magazine, never letting the case out of his sight. When an attractive young lady in a business suit came into the room and called his name, he stood and followed her down a long corridor and into a massive conference room with a table large enough to accommodate 12 padded chairs that slid easily beneath.

Tracy plopped down in one of the chairs, and after declining an offer of water or coffee, he settled in, as the young woman left him alone to stare out the window across the way. But there wasn't much time for contemplating. In less than a minute, three men in expensive-looking suits and grim faces entered the conference room and took seats at the head of the table, as far away from Tracy as possible. The move said volumes. Once seated, all three turned to Tracy with questioning looks that were meant to make Tracy squirm. It didn't work. One of them spoke with an air of authority.

"Detective Tracy, I am Charles Gibbons, one of the senior partners here at O.G.G. I understand that you are here on behalf of Davis Runyon?"

Tracy swallowed before answering. "Yes, sir, I am. I have a proposal, and..."

"Let me stop you right there, Detective. We don't make deals. We are not negotiators on any level. Mr. Davis

47

Runyon stole money from this company over 11 years ago...”

“And he paid for his crime, sir. He served his time and was a model prisoner, according to his record.”

Charles Gibbons smiled for the first time. Tracy was thinking he would hate to see the man’s dental bill. “Model prisoner or not, we do not make deals with individuals who steal from our firm, Detective. He was a trusted employee who betrayed our trust. There is no excuse good enough. We prosecuted eleven years ago because we wanted justice.”

“Justice,” Detective Tracy stated, “is something you get in a perfect world. Here, we have the law.”

Tracy pushed his chair back, stood, and moved down the long table until he was standing behind an empty chair next to one of the three gentlemen. He had been at the “kid’s end of the table” long enough. He pulled out the chair and slid himself under as he set the attaché case next to him.

“I don’t like shouting, gentlemen. My first round of questions was not about what you do or do not do. The first round of questions tells me what I am dealing with. And now that I know, I am not asking you to exonerate him, Mr. Gibbons; I am asking you to forgive him. There’s a difference. I know all about the civil lawsuit your firm has filed against Mr. Runyon. I am here to offer you what you are suing for.”

All three men turned to one another. After a moment, the furtive looks that passed between the three dissipated, and they turned back to Tracy. The man on Tracy’s left spoke for the first time. “What is your offer, Detective? Or should I say, what is Mr. Runyon’s offer?”

“It’s simple. He pays back the $234,000 he took from the company, and you drop the lawsuit against him and sign some sort of document saying that you are satisfied with the return of the money and that you won't prosecute him later."

Once again, the three men stared at each other without speaking before turning back. "Are you telling us that Mr. Runyon still has the money?"

"Yes. He never spent a penny. It has been buried in his sister's backyard for over 11 years. She had no knowledge of the money; she is not an accomplice or anything, just an unknowing guardian."

The third man, yet unspoken, suddenly found his voice. "I am going to go and consult with the firm's legal counsel, Detective. I will be right back."

When the man left the room, there was dead silence until he returned with an important-looking man in tow. He introduced Tracy to the man, whose name was Bertrand Carter, apparently a mouthpiece for the firm.

"Detective, I understand that Mr. Runyon is willing to pay back in full the money he stole, down to the last penny... if we are willing to drop the lawsuit. Is that correct?"

"Yes, sir."

"And you are speaking for Mr. Runyon?"

"Yes. And I am prepared to make that payment. Today."

Tracy set the attaché case on the table, entered the combination, and opened the top. Inside were rows and rows of $100 bills.

"The only stipulation being, Mr. Carter, that you leave this money inside your safe here at the firm until the lawsuit against Mr. Runyon has been dismissed and he has proof of the dismissal, and the letter he has requested is in his hands."

Bertrand Carter looked to the head of the table, where Mr. Charles Gibbons gave a nod of consent. He then turned back to Tracy. "Okay, Detective. We consent. The money will remain in the safe, and we will provide Mr. Runyon proof of the dismissal and the letter."

Tracy wrote some information on a pad of paper sitting on the table and handed it to Mr. Carter. "This is Mr. Runyon's present address. The name of the firm in which he is currently employed is The Courier Agency. They know all about his past. In fact, that's why they hired him. He is considered an expert on company theft for obvious reasons."

Tracy stood and moved towards the door with Mr. Carter and the case of money beside him. He turned left towards the elevator as Carter and the case turned right to a set of offices. Once back on the street, Tracy smiled to himself. His good deed for the day—maybe for the year.

* * *

"Nothing is more creative…than a brilliant mind with a purpose." —D. Brown

Eight days before the arrest of Mary Trotter

Detective Tracy looked up in time to see a face he had only seen once in the last eleven years. The face of a man he had helped put in prison. It's not every cop who wants to see the men they have incarcerated, but this man was an exception. And even though it was Tracy who helped catch and convict the man, he had empathy for someone he considered a "true genius."

Tracy stood and offered his hand to the short, well-muscled man whose persona was in direct contradiction to his clothing: a suit that was way too snug and a large bow tie of yellow and green print. He looked like a kid's show host on the way to Sunday prayer meetin', who pulled his little brother's suit out of the closet by mistake.

Tracy began the conversation. "Hello, Mr. Davis Runyon. I'm glad you suggested this lunch. I wouldn't have missed it."

The little man smiled. Slowly. He set the attaché case he was carrying on the floor next to him. "Detective Tracy. Hope you don't mind that incident the other night, the pop in the jaw. I'm sorry."

"No, you're not."

"Well, I have to admit I had been waiting eleven years to do that. Thought about it every night in prison. In fact, just before lights out, I said your name five times."

"I'm sure you did."

Tracy eyed the man's biceps bulging inside the tightly stretched suit. "And it seems you haven't exactly been idle while you were away."

"No, I haven't, Detective. White-collar criminals have advantages. There was a small gym and a boxing training camp. It kept me busy. I got out eleven years into a fifteen-year stretch on the old 'good behavior' statute. But we are not here to talk about the last eleven years; we are here to talk about the next eleven."

Davis Runyon picked up the saltshaker from the table—the one that was holding the plastic-covered menu and stained with coffee and grape jelly—upright.

"I want you to help me with something, Detective. You don't owe me, I know that. And I realize that back eleven years ago, you were just doing your job that the city of New York pays you to do, as meager as that pay must be. But I'm asking you for this favor out of the kindness of your heart. I saw you sitting in the courtroom during my trial. I could see that you actually cared."

Well, he was right. "So what is it you want me to do, Mr. Runyon? And please tell me it's legal."

Runyon replaced the saltshaker and the menu. It was as if he had been holding onto them like a security blanket until he heard Tracy's answer.

"I want you to return the money I stole from the firm. I have it here in my case... all of it. But I do have a few terms."

"Wait, are you telling me, Mr. Runyon, that you have the money that you stole—the $230,000?"

"$234,000, Detective. I put the money in a strong box and buried it in my sister's backyard when I realized you were getting close. The police never found the box; I hid it well. And my sister had no idea it was there. In fact, I didn't tell anyone. But now Oppenheimer, Goldberg, and Gibbons have filed a civil lawsuit against me. And I want them to drop the case. I have a good job now, Detective. The company I work for has hired me on as an expert. And I have to say I am."

"What does this company do?"

"Other firms hire us to find internal crooks— employees who are cooking the books, so to speak. Stealing. And believe me, I know all the schemes. I know how to spot the signs. And they pay me well."

Tracy felt the man's mood had changed in the last few moments. It was time to ask the tough questions. "And you believe that you will be satisfied with your present salary? You can live on the wages you make? You won't need to find a way to...?"

"Yes, Detective. Just because my name will follow the word felon in my obituary doesn't necessarily mean that I can't change or see the light. Seems that once upon a time, in a 10x10 jail cell, I discovered that I can live modestly. I no longer need finer things—the gravy to put on the meat. I'm even thinking about looking up my old girlfriend, Ann Beasley. I think she is still living over in Brooklyn on State Street."

Tracy had a few more questions. And he wanted to hear the terms that Runyon had selected. Over burgers and fries, the two men discussed the plan of attack on

Oppenheimer, Goldberg, and Gibbons. It was going to be simple and straightforward. Nothing but the truth.

When lunch was over, Tracy shook hands with Davis Runyon and then turned to go. (Runyon had insisted on paying for lunch. And Tracy let him.) He was leaving with a good feeling and a case full of money. $234,700, to be exact. And he didn't plan on letting the attaché out of his sight. The next order of business was to make an appointment with Oppenheimer, Goldberg, and Gibbons. The sooner, the better.

Tracy headed toward the exit leading to the sidewalk. With his free hand, he pushed open the door and looked back to see Runyon watching him. Runyon waved and smiled as Tracy stepped out into the sunlight with a light-hearted step. What he didn't see? He didn't see the smile slowly fade from Davis Runyon's face, as he watched the man who would set him free from the invisible prison of his own making, disappear from sight. The smile that slowly turned into a sneer.

* * *

"Men who are very cool but also brilliant, they are almost always insane." —J. Blalock

Twelve days before the arrest of Mary Trotter

Tracy was staring at some old court records in the case of *The State versus Runyon*. He remembered. It had been eleven years. An open-and-shut case. A man with the name he didn't deserve, Davis Harvey Runyon, was stealing money from the firm he worked for. He was an accounting assistant. No one important. No big salary or job title. One day, the firm found out something was wrong with the books. There was a scramble in the accounting department. No one could quite figure out who and how.

It was 1968, the year Tracy had received his gold shield, moving from police officer to detective third class. A big step after years on the force. He was excited. Enthusiastic. A rookie detective with a lot of miles to go. And a friend of his was an employee of the firm where this Runyon worked—Oppenheimer, Goldberg, and Gibbons. His friend was nervous when H.R. began the internal investigation. He didn't want to be accused of something he didn't do. Or worse, get fired. So this friend came to Tracy and asked for help. He knew Tracy was good at investigation. And he was right.

Tracy remembered reading about an accountant who stole money from a law firm by changing the amount of the monthly tax payments. The books were never wrong because they matched the bank statements each month. So, no one ever caught on. Until someone did.

When Tracy suggested to his friend that the firm look into the tax account... voilà, there was the discrepancy. Bigger than life. But no one would have found it unless they knew to look back into the previous month's filings. When they discovered who filed the taxes—a lowly, menial job that was so simple it was given to an accounting clerk by the name of Davis Runyon—then it was apparent where the thief was hiding. Right under their noses.

The firm filed charges against Runyon. They wanted him prosecuted. Runyon didn't put up a defense. And he refused to return the money. Said he spent it but couldn't produce any evidence. No receipts for any big purchases, no large amounts in or out of his meager bank account. The firm was sure he still had the money hidden somewhere.

Runyon was convicted and sentenced to fifteen years. Tracy remembered no one came to the trial. But he did. He sat in on the proceedings. He somehow liked Davis Runyon. Admired his brilliance. The meek little man that no one suspects, who almost got away with it. But Davis

Runyon hadn't counted on the rookie detective with the NYC force, who was about to become one helluva investigator. Where was the brilliance now? Tracy picked up the phone and made a few calls. He wanted to track down Runyon. And he would.

* * *

"He has a brilliant mind until he makes it up."
—M. Asquith

Thirteen days before the arrest of Mary Trotter

Detective Tracy was sitting in his office. He called in one of his fellow detectives, Jim Bell. Bell had a memory that was famous around the precinct. He could remember details of cases from years back. When Jim Bell entered Tracy's office, he sat down in the nearby chair, a toothpick sticking through his mouth—a remnant from lunch.

"Hey, Bell, do you remember when we first made gold shield?"

"Like it was yesterday."

"Remember this case... forgery? The perp was stealing money through the tax account. Little guy, big firm."

"Yeah, I remember. What about him?"

"Do you remember the guy's name? I think he had two last names. Like his first name was a last name. Something like that."

"Davis. Davis was the first name. Can't remember the last."

"Runyon," said Tracy. "Davis Runyon—yeah, that's it. I am going to check through the system and see if he has gotten out of the pen recently."

Jim Bell started to leave and then turned back. He seemed to have noticed something.

"What's that bruise on your face, Tracy? Some sweet little lady getting a bit too physical?"

Tracy worked his jaw back and forth. "Actually, some guy came up to the table and popped me in the mouth last night while my date and I were having dinner over on the west side. And I think it might be this Runyon guy. But I'm just not sure. He looked different somehow. Bigger. Think I will look into the files and then check with the D.A.'s office." Tracy looked out his small window, contemplating. "Who knows, Jim? Maybe I'm wasting my time, and this will all be for nothing."

* * *

EPILOGUE

"All of us get brilliant ideas, only a few have the courage to take the next step."—M. Arora

Eleven years earlier

Davis Runyon stared at the last form of identification he had established: a driver's license with the name Ralph Rivers. He had started with the first letter of the alphabet for the first bank deposit and had carried on until the 18th letter and the 18th bank. He was now on the letter R—double R. Each of the names had been a double: Alan Anderson. Bart Bradley. Carl Carpenter. And so on.

Easier to remember. And remember, he must, as nothing could be written down. Anywhere. Davis Runyon was an accounting clerk who had slowly embezzled money from the firm where he went to work every day—Oppenheimer, Goldberg, and Gibbons. He was not the head accountant; no, he was just an assistant. But a brilliant one that everyone overlooked and stepped over each day on their way to the top. The theft was easy for Davis and his brilliant mind. He did it slowly so no one particular audit would be his downfall. And the company's bank statements always matched the company records. It was all done through the tax reports. Every report was increased by just so much as to go undetected. The extra amount went into Davis Runyon's suit pants and then into one of the many bank accounts until $13,000 was reached. (Davis Runyon was brilliant, but he was also eccentric and quirky. And 13 was his favorite number.) If all the accounts had the same amount, it was easy to remember.

So far, Davis had accumulated $234,000. Eighteen different bank branches and other financial institutions, with $13,000 in each one. And now they were all accumulating interest. It had taken Davis several years, but he felt secure, safe. He had even requested that no bank statements be sent to his apartment each month. Mail could fall into the wrong hands—nosy neighbors, etc. So he opened a P.O. box and always used the P.O. number as an address.

And each time, when he was ready, he went to his favorite forger, Mary Trotter, and established a new identity. He then put the new driver's license, passport, and bank book in a box he kept hidden in his sister's basement—a steel box with a combination lock that was impenetrable. Yes, he felt safe and secure. Until.

Someone had uncovered a discrepancy in the books. Davis Runyon was about to be questioned by a rookie detective on the NYC police force by the name of Nick Tracy. Davis Runyon was brilliant, but someone had said that Tracy was brilliant, too. Cop brilliant. And the firm was about to find out that their lowly accounting assistant had been stealing from them for years. The heads of the firm were talking about prosecuting. And prosecute, they would. Davis Runyon was about to be convicted and incarcerated for eleven years. The judge would hand down a sentence of 15 years, but Runyon would get a few years shaved off for good behavior. Sometimes, it pays to be nice, and Davis Runyon was a nice guy. And while in prison, Runyon was going to do two things without fail:

1.) To the annoyance of the other prisoners, Davis Runyon was going to switch the channel on the communal television once a week to catch the financial report sometime during the morning news. It cost him a few cartons of cigarettes each week, but it was worth it. Because Davis would be going back to his cell where he kept his papers, and he would calculate how much compound interest he had accumulated that week. The Feds had been on a "stop and go" monetary spree for quite some time, and the interest rates had climbed steadily until the climbing had stopped and the soaring had begun. Whereas 1970 had started with a 6% rate, 1974 saw an increase to 11%. Then 1979 had peaked at 16%. By Davis Runyon's estimation—and if the Feds' track record held—1980 would soon bring a whopping 20%. And Davis Runyon had been making money with every increase. A lot of money. If his calculations were correct—and of course they were—he had more than doubled his money on a compounded annual basis.

2.) The other thing he had been doing each and every evening was to recite a list of the 18 bank branches and financial institutions where the money was located and the identity he had used for each one. Just so he would never forget which identity went with which bank. Alan Anderson, Mercantile Bank / 51st Street Branch. Bart Bradley, M.O.N.Y. / Broadway Branch. Carl Carpenter, National Bank / Park Avenue Branch. And so on. Eighteen identities and eighteen locations. And when he was done reciting, he would say the name of that brilliant rookie cop who had been the catalyst to get him sent away: Detective Nick Tracy.

When Davis Runyon had his early release in 1979, he would have more than enough money—over and above the original $234,000 that he stole. Runyon was going to see to it that he was comfortable for the rest of his natural life, because he had studied the market and read every book that dealt with finance he could get his hands on in the prison library. There was no longer a need to steal. He could use the interest money to make more money through investments. Yes, if everything went as planned, Davis Runyon would be secure financially.

But Runyon knew that there was one thing he wanted to do after he was released from the white-collar prison where he had spent the last eleven years. He had thought about it for every one of those 4,015 days he had been locked up like an animal. He wanted to find that cop, Nick Tracy, who had figured out the one weak link in his plan, and give Tracy a punch in the mouth. When Runyon wasn't reading and honing his financial skills in prison, he had been working out in the prison gym.)

...And then, after this, Detective Tracy came looking for him—as Runyon was sure he would—he would use Tracy like an unsuspecting pawn to get the firm he had worked for to drop the charges against him. He would coerce Tracy into convincing Oppenheimer, Goldberg, and Gibbons that the money had been buried in his sister's backyard all these eleven years. (Who wouldn't believe a nice, smart cop with a clean record?) They could have their old dusty money back, because now Runyon had more than enough for what he wanted to do.

But Davis Runyon, in his brilliant mind, had made one mistake. And it was a critical one. Yes, the only thing that Davis Runyon hadn't counted on... was Mary Trotter. Mary was the only person in the world who knew about the 18 different identities... as she was the one who forged each and every one. Eighteen different forgeries; eighteen different forms of identity. And in her own brilliant mind, Mary Trotter had figured out exactly what Runyon was doing. Davis Runyon wasn't the only one watching the market and what the Feds were doing. The interest rate was a constant topic at Mary Trotter's dinner table.

Now, it had been just a matter of waiting until Davis Runyon got out of prison and collected all the original money and all the earnings from all the locations. And then, when Runyon had all that money in his possession—all that beautiful cash—then, and only then, would Mary find him and blackmail him for half the money. She would have him bring the money to his workplace after hours, knowing full well that Runyon wouldn't dare resist, or she would blow the whistle, and he would be out all the money. And if he resisted... then ruthless Mary Trotter, who had no qualms about committing crimes and doing time, wouldn't hesitate to... Well, you already know the rest.

THE NOTE, THE YACHT, AND THE BESSERMANS

PROLOGUE

Somewhere in the Hamptons, Long Island

Sally Myerson stepped into the passenger's side of the small sports car. The car was fresh off the showroom floor—a brand-new 1979 model that was candy apple red with a rag top and an interior the color of an Englishman's saddle. And it was expensive. Sally glanced to her left, eyeing the young lady who would soon be turning over the ignition and driving her (at a breakneck speed, if past trips were any indication) to her house, where Sally would be deposited at the front door of her small home with the green trim and the sapphire blue awnings. It was these late-night working hours that were the most trying part of Sally's job. Most days, she would finish at a decent hour and be able to catch the train home. Then, at other times, like tonight, she would have to rely on someone in the Besserman household to drive her. And that, more often than not, meant Lydia, her boss's young daughter, who did not like to obey posted speed limits (they weren't there for her) or take precautions around the sharp curves down the long stretch of road.

Sally mulled over her options. Should she close her eyes and just pray for a safe journey? Should she grip the armrest, like she normally did, and hang on for dear life? Or should she jump out of the car and demand that a taxi be called for her?

Sally made her decision. A decision that would change everything. She buckled up her safety belt and hesitated for just a moment, lingering in that gap between thought and action. Before young Lydia could turn over the key, Sally looked back at the large two-story house behind them. The shade was pulled on the upper window. It was the window in the room where Sally worked every day with the owner of the house—Arnold Besserman.

Sally let out a scream. She clutched desperately at Lydia's arm, tugging on her shirt. "Lydia, look... at the study window. Look! Someone is hitting someone."

Lydia, all of twenty-five years old, turned in her seat to look back at the house. She let out a stifled scream. "Oh, no. Daddy!"

Within seconds, both women were running up the long-sloped driveway and then turning onto the steps that led up to the big house. They reached the front door and began pounding. Lydia was the most vocal. "Brooks, let us in! Brooks. Someone come quick. Let us in!"

To Sally, it seemed like hours, but perhaps it was only seconds before Brooks threw open the door. "Great Caesar's ghost, what in the world is going on, Miss Lydia? Why are you...?"

But neither woman gave the houseman a chance to ask any further questions. Lydia flew past Brooks and took the stairs up to the landing, two at a time. Sally stayed right on her heels. Both women arrived at the study door simultaneously. Lydia reached for the handle first and turned, but nothing happened.

Sally knew exactly what to do. "Let me get the key," she called out as she ran for the hall table, while behind her back, she could hear Lydia pounding on the door and screaming for her father to "open up." When Sally found the key, she ran back to the study and handed it to a very distraught Lydia, who inserted the key and turned the knob. The door opened instantly. And when they entered the room, they found Arnold Besserman stretched out on the Persian carpet, his scalp bleeding from a wound to the back of the head. The fire poker from the set of fireplace andirons was lying next to him. The sharp end of the poker was covered with blood and tissue.

Lydia screamed. "Daaadddy..." and started to run to her father.

But Sally held her back. "Don't touch him, Lydia. Don't touch anything. Let me just check his pulse. Go over to the phone on the desk and call for the police and an ambulance. Hurry."

Lydia, seemingly in shock, did as she was told. Sally started to reach down and grab her employer's wrist; her whole body was shaking, and her forehead was wet with perspiration. But before she could do anything, she glanced back to where Brooks was standing there in the doorway—ever-steady Brooks, who suddenly had found his voice and his senses.

"Please come out of there, Miss Sally. Don't touch him. I will tend to Mr. Besserman. I will see what I can do. Please come out, both of you."

Sally Myerson, the good employee that she was, listened to what Brooks had to say. Maybe the man was right. Best not to touch anything. And with a nod of her head, she grabbed Lydia and complied with the houseman's request. Sally guided the sobbing young woman through the study doorway she herself traveled in and out of every day for fourteen years, just as the sound of a siren could be heard turning onto the long driveway of the Besserman estate. And that's when Sally Myerson passed out cold on the blue-patterned carpet.

* * *

*"If I doubt your intentions, I will
never trust your actions." —C. Wallace*

Detective Nick Tracy of the New York City Police Department was once again assisting the Long Island precinct, and he was available when the call came into the station that warm spring night. The acting chief informed him that there had been a murder at one of the mansions there in the Hamptons. After making note of the address and the time, Tracy gathered his things and headed for the door. The night was clear, and the moon was full as the detective made his way to the scene of the murder.

And... These were simply the first moments of a case that Nick Tracy would refer to in years to come as *The Note, the Yacht, and the Bessermans*. It wasn't going to be a particularly notorious case—no scandalous details for the local Hampton residents to mull over, dissect, and gossip about. Nothing like the infamous John Roth case. But there were going to be so many ins and outs, twists and turns, that no one involved would ever forget even one detail. Least of all, Detective Tracy.

* * *

The big house was lit up like a Christmas tree. All of the outside floodlights were on, as well as the low driveway lights. The first to arrive on the scene were doing their job as Tracy was led inside the house by a man named Brooks. Tracy didn't know if that was the man's last name or first name. Not that it mattered—first or last. He looked like a Brooks. He informed Tracy, as they walked, that he was the houseman, sort of a modern-day butler; he kept the

64

household running, monitored the cook and the maid, answered the door and the phone, filled the gas tanks of each of the cars— "that sort of thing."

As they approached the study door, Tracy asked a pointed question, and Brooks quickly recited a list of the Besserman occupants, all six of whom resided upstairs and all of whom were home during the time of the murder:

1.) Arnold Besserman, age 55 (victim): a famous author of several books, all fiction and all bestselling. Most were highly anticipated before they even hit bookstore shelves.
2.) Arnold's wife, Andrea Besserman, age 50: did little or nothing, depending on her whim that day.
3.) Their daughter, Lydia Besserman, age 25: engaged to be married. (According to the houseman, Lydia was in no hurry and much enjoyed the life that wealth offered her.)
4.) Adam Besserman, Arnold's younger brother, age 51: had fallen on hard times and needed to live there with his brother to reestablish a hold on life and get back on his feet.
5.) Bebee Besserman, Adam's wife, age 42: had snagged Adam when she was his secretary. According to Brooks, the first Mrs. Besserman had protested little.
6.) And last but not least—Brenda Peters, age 58: nurse to the late Besserman matriarch (Arnold and Adam's deceased aunt). Brenda was now part of the house and handed out medical advice to the entire Besserman clan. Interestingly enough, she now resided in her late patient's room.

Of the downstairs residents, there were three, all employed in one capacity or another by the family:
1.) Brooks, the houseman

2.) Sarina, the household maid
3.) "Chilly," the cook

In addition, there were two people who were usually in the house at one time or another:
    1.) Sally Meyerson, age 53: Mr. Arnold Besserman's assistant and secretary
    2.) Paul Marx, age 26: Miss Lydia Besserman's fiancé

Tracy made a few notes in his book and tried to keep up with the fast-talking Brooks. They were headed into the study, where the forensics boys had already examined the body, taken fingerprints, bagged the murder weapon, and gathered any pertinent evidence. Now it was up to Tracy to fill in the missing gaps. Create a case.

When they reached the study, Tracy asked Brooks to "hang back" and let him go in alone, which he did. Tracy closed the door. The medical examiner was the first to respond to Tracy's questions.

"Pretty cut and dry, Detective. The victim was hit in the back of the head with the fireplace poker. He didn't stand a chance. There are traces of hair, blood, and tissue covering the end. I'm sure the boys in the lab will determine they all belong to the deceased. And I hate to say it, but it looks like the handle has been wiped clean. Doubt they'll find any prints, but I'm sure you'll have them go through the motions."

"Okay, Karl. Thank you. As you probably know, I'm helping out the L.I. division. They're short-handed. Give me an autopsy report as soon as you have it."

The M.E. nodded and went back to work on the body of Arnold Besserman, checking the man over before allowing the boys to move him. As Tracy crossed the wood-paneled study, the medical examiner called out.

"Forgot to mention, Detective... two of the people in the house saw the killer and Mr. Besserman outlined on the window shade, struggling. They were down in the driveway. It's going to pinpoint the time of death for us. But I'll verify that after I run a few tests."

Tracy nodded a silent response as he checked all the windows—every one of them locked securely. He then checked the shades, which were all drawn. Next, he looked around for secret panels, of which there were none. (That would have made his job too easy.) No, there was only one way in and out of this study, and that was through the single door.

Tracy left the study and headed back to see the houseman, Brooks. He had decided to take a few minutes and conduct a little interview with the two people who saw the murder happen from the driveway below. The efficient Mr. Brooks would know where to find them both.

* * *

"No use pretending to do good in front of people who are doing the same." —*R. Sharma*

Tracy sat opposite Miss Lydia Besserman and Miss Sally Myerson in the mansion's living room, with its twelve-foot ceilings and pillow-covered sofas. He had been introduced to both women by Brooks, who had left the room discreetly after filling him in with a few details. Now, he was looking for clarification as to where they were when they saw the murder occur. He started with the victim's twenty-five-year-old daughter.

Lydia Besserman was attractive in a gothic sort of way. Tracy noticed the long, pointed fingernails with the dark polish and the black-cherry lipstick first. She would have been perfect in a Bela Lugosi vampire movie. The Besserman daughter was thin and willowy. Her clothes were on the eccentric, anti-establishment side. And she had a couple of nervous tics; her hand jerked back and forth when she wasn't running it through her long black hair, and she blinked hard every few minutes with a certain regularity. Tracy hoped his opening questions wouldn't increase her stress.

"I wonder if you could please tell me what transpired here tonight, Miss Besserman. Brooks has told me that you were starting to drive away from the house when you saw your father and someone struggling here in the study. Their outlines were on the shade?"

"Yes, Detective. I had just started the car..."

The woman sitting beside Lydia interrupted. "No, Lydia. You hadn't started the car yet."

"Oh, that's right, Sally. Correction, Detective. I was just starting the car when I looked back and saw the outline on the shade. Someone was striking my father with the fireplace poker."

"What made you so sure that it was your father? Maybe your father was the one doing the striking. Or maybe he wasn't even in the room. How could you be certain it wasn't two other members of the family who were in the study?"

"You're right. I guess I just assumed it was Daddy since it was his office, and he rarely let anyone come in. But of course, I wasn't positive. Not until Sally and I ran upstairs and entered the study." Lydia Besserman's eyes filled with tears. And then she blinked hard... again. "And there was Daddy on the floor. Dead."

"Could you identify the man struggling with your father?"

"No. He was just an outline." The other woman in the room reached over and put her arm around Lydia Besserman as the younger woman dissolved into tears. Tracy wasn't sure if he would get anything further out of the Besserman girl. He gave a jerk of his head in the direction of the door, and Sally Myerson got the message. She led Lydia Besserman out and passed her off to Brooks.

Tracy noticed that Sally Myerson walked with a decided limp. She then returned to the room and sat down in the chair she had occupied a moment before. Sally Myerson was a tall, fifty-something woman with a thin frame, mousy brown hair, and dark, expressive eyebrows that ran in a straight line across her hazel-green eyes. A Claudette Colbert character messing with Clark Gable's libido in *It Happened One Night.* And she was plain. Her face was void of makeup, her hair was haphazardly combed and pulled back into a loose ponytail, and if she had any figure at all, it was buried inside her clothes, which hung on her body two sizes too big. It was almost as if she purposely dressed to disguise the fact that she was way more attractive than she appeared. Even the lilt of Sally Myerson's voice was pleasant but firm—like good strawberry Jell-O.

"What Lydia said is correct, Detective. That just about covers it. What else could you possibly want to know?"

"Well, for starters, when you got to the study door, what did you find?"

"What do you mean?"

"Was the door wide open, closed?"

"Oh, I see. It was closed. Locked. I retrieved the key from the hall table. In one of the top drawers."

"Did you find that odd, Miss Myerson?"

"Yes. But on occasion, Arnold would lock himself in when he was working, so as not to be disturbed by other family members."

"I'm curious, Miss Myerson. What did you do for Mr. Besserman? Brooks mentioned you were an assistant of some sort."

"Yes, Detective. I guess you could say that. I took notes for Arnold, transcribed those notes, and edited his manuscripts for punctuation, phrasing, and content. I gave him ideas, quotes, alternate endings, and helped to write everything he ever published." Sally Myerson frowned and swept her hair away from her eyes. Definitely a C. Colbert move. "I guess you could say I was more Arnold Besserman than Arnold Besserman."

Detective Nick Tracy smiled. He liked this woman. If she was willing to help, she might be the perfect one to assist him in getting to the bottom of who struck and killed her boss—even though she was probably headed to the unemployment line.

"It sounds like your picture should have been on those book jackets, Ms. Myerson. You certainly are prettier than Mr. Besserman. But after all the events unfolding tonight in this house... I guess this means you're out of a job."

Was Sally Myerson blushing? Maybe. "Well, the thing is, Detective, I think the family will keep me on for at least several more years. Arnold and I recently finished three new outlines. Andrea, Arnold's wife, needs me to sort everything out. Like I said, there is enough material for three more books. Posthumously, of course. That will keep me busy for quite some time."

"Does the family know that you were basically a ghostwriter for Mr. Besserman?"

"Yes. They know. And they also know that I don't mind. I am paid extremely well, Detective. I made almost as much as Arnold. It was always a dual collaboration that was mutually agreed upon before we started working together fourteen years ago. I have become like a spinster aunt to everyone in the Besserman family. They love me, and the feeling is mutual. I think my position here is pretty secure."

"Okay, Miss Myerson. Because of your fondness for the Besserman family, perhaps you would do me a favor and be my guide through this process of meeting the family."

"Certainly, Detective. I'm glad to help."

"Good. But first, I have a few questions. I am assuming that you saw the person on the shade also?"

"Yes, I did. He or she was about the same size as Arnold."

"He or she? So it was possible that it was a woman?"

"Yes, Detective. It's definitely possible."

"Okay, what can you tell me about the hours preceding the murder?"

"We started work at 10 a.m., as usual. We were working on some editing. Mr. Besserman had one visitor around one o'clock. I had never seen the man before. His name was Delbert Moore, and he worked at the local synagogue. He said he found a letter in one of the synagogue books written by Marion Besserman, Arnold's late aunt. She died a few months ago aboard the family yacht during a violent storm. She was swept overboard, according to the family members on the yacht that night."

"Did you see the note, Miss Myerson? If so, what did it say?"

"Arnold was very upset when he read the letter. Like he had seen a ghost. I hate to admit it, but when he showed Mr. Moore out, I read the letter. It was sitting on the desk; I couldn't help myself."

"What did the note say?"

Sally Myerson took a deep, steadying breath. It looked as though it hurt. "It said something like... *If I die any time soon, please look to my nephew Arnold Besserman. Especially if I die on the yacht this weekend—it may be made to look like an accident. Arnold is out to get my money. His damn books are running dry.* And it was signed by Marion Besserman and dated the day before the fatal yacht trip."

"What happened to the letter?"

Sally Myerson took another deep breath. She was obviously a secret keeper, and this tell-all went against her nature. "Arnold threw it in the fireplace and then set it on fire. If you go back into the study, Detective, I'm sure you will find the ashes. The fireplace was cleaned last week. It will be the only thing there."

"Did you hear Mr. Moore try to blackmail Mr. Besserman?"

"No. I did not. Perhaps Mr. Moore didn't know what was inside the envelope. I don't think he ever opened it. When he handed it to Arnold, it was sealed. And the only writing on the outside of the envelope said: *To Whom It May Concern, from M. Besserman.* Mr. Moore said he knew Marion was Arnold's aunt, so he brought it right away."

"What was Mr. Besserman's reaction after he burned the note?"

"No reaction. But I will tell you this: a few months ago, Arnold was thinking about writing a novel based on the night his aunt died. A mystery. And everyone in the family knew it. And I don't believe that Arnold killed his aunt. Marion Besserman was a bit paranoid. The fact that she went up on that deck during a storm is proof that she was not thinking clearly. And Arnold announced one night at dinner that he had scrapped the mystery. And just in case you need to know, Detective, of the three future books that Arnold and I have outlined... one is a book about espionage and two are action thrillers. So if someone did push the old girl over the railing, no one needed to silence Arnold."

"But someone did, Miss Myerson. Do you have any thoughts as to who would want your boss dead? Maybe someone outside the house?"

"No. He doesn't have any enemies. Except..."

"Yes?"

"Well, it's really not that important. But he did have an argument recently with a fellow author. Mr. Jamison McNalley. McNalley accused Arnold of plagiarizing his book from a few years back. It's not true, of course. Arnold didn't need to plagiarize anyone. He had lots of ideas. He threw them out left and right. I fielded most and turned them into words. That's kind of how we worked. But of course, Jamison McNalley didn't believe a word of it."

"Where would I find this Jamison McNalley?"

"Not far from here, Detective. At least not far from here tomorrow. There is a book signing at a major bookstore in town. I can give you the information."

"That would be helpful, Miss Myerson. And I will be back in the morning to interview the family members. If you will please make sure that everyone is assembled in the living room, I would appreciate it."

With that, Tracy left the room and went to speak briefly to the remainder of the family, who had presumably been tucked away somewhere in the house when the murder occurred. One by one, they reassured Tracy that they would help in any way they could and that they didn't know why anyone would do such a thing. Of course, one of them was lying. Or worse—one of them could be a cold-blooded killer.

* * *

"Wonder which face she sees when she looks in the mirror?" —*C. Joy Bell*

At 9 a.m. the next morning, Tracy walked through the front door of the Besserman home with a patrolman by his side—the same patrolman he had worked with on the John Roth case. A bit of familiarity. There was something about this house... other than the fact that the Howell mansion was not far down the road. Maybe it was because,

73

like before, he was on loan to the Long Island precinct. Mere coincidence. No time for reminiscing—moving on.

Tracy went straight to the living room, where he found the entire household gathered. Some were sipping coffee, and some were nibbling on pastries provided by Chilly, the Jamaican cook. Most were sitting with their hands resting on their laps, waiting—obviously—for him. "Good morning, everyone. As I stated last night, I'm Detective Nicholas Tracy, and I am here to find out who murdered Mr. Besserman. I need to rely on your memory and what you did or didn't see last night before Mr. Besserman was attacked."

Tracy turned to the woman on his right. She was hard to miss. Sally Myerson had described her to a tee. She was perfect in every way and very much playing the part of the grieving widow. "Mrs. Besserman, I'll start with you. If you could please follow me into the dining room."

Andrea Besserman was a modern-looking woman with a trendy hairstyle (not a root showing), the latest in couture clothing, and impeccable makeup (not an eyelash uncurled). She was attractive, but not beautiful. As Tracy would soon find out, Andrea Besserman was *vogue* on the outside but *vague* on the inside. And she never left the house looking like anyone other than Andrea Besserman. She began her monologue with tears standing in her swollen red eyes. "Oh, what a stir you are causing, Detective. I understand you have to question everyone, but do you really believe I could have killed Arnie in such a brutal way? Ridiculous. I could never overpower anyone on the plus side of sixty pounds."

"I'm not accusing anyone, Mrs. Besserman. I just wanted to start with you because I was hoping you might have some idea as to who would like to see your husband dead."

"The idea is absurd, of course. My late husband was a friend to all and an enemy to none. He was jovial, talented, generous, and a good husband and father. Who would want to see a man like that dead?"

"Well, someone did."

"I suppose Sally told you about Jamison McNalley. He is quite a bully. But I doubt he would have the smarts to kill anyone. He can write books, but he wouldn't have the stamina to climb up the trellis out there and sneak into Arnie's study and kill him. He would be more likely to send a poison dart from some ancient African tribe. He does travel to the dark continent a great deal."

"Did you see or talk to the gentleman who showed up here yesterday?"

Tracy consulted his notes. "A Mr. Delbert Moore, who works at the synagogue."

"No. I didn't see Mr. Moore. What did he want with Arnold?" (The dead husband had gone from *Arnie* to *Arnold* in a matter of seconds.)

"He found a note written by Mr. Besserman's aunt. A Marion Besserman."

Andrea Besserman looked taken aback. She clutched at her silk blouse with one hand. "Aunt Marion died at sea a few months ago, Detective. A boating accident during a violent storm. When did she write this so-called note?"

"Before the trip."

Andrea Besserman's eyes never left Tracy's. She looked as if she wanted to start crying once more. She stopped clutching at her blouse and let her hand fall—as if she were dismissing the incident altogether. "What else do you need to know, Detective?"

"Are you aware of any means into or out of the study other than through the door?"

"No."

"How does the door lock?"

"From the inside. There is a key we keep in the hall table, in case it accidentally gets locked."

"So someone inside the room would have to physically lock the door from the inside?"

"Yes. There is a button on the doorknob."

"So whoever killed Mr. Besserman locked the door when they left the room?"

"If it was locked, yes. That is the only way I know of."

"Unless, of course, Mr. Besserman locked the door himself when the killer came into the room so as not to be disturbed. And then the killer left the room by other means. Now, this is a very delicate question, Mrs. Besserman, but do you know anyone who resides in this house who would want to kill your husband?"

"No, Detective. I don't. We all loved him. He wrote his books, sent them to his publisher, and then went on to the next book. That was what he did. Harmless."

"Okay. Thank you, Mrs. Besserman. Please send in your husband's brother, Adam, and his wife."

* * *

"If they talk about other people with you, they talk about you with other people." —C. Wallace

Adam and Bebee Besserman were like opposing pole magnets. They seemed to repel each other by just being in the same room at the same time. One sat on one side of the dining room table while the other one sat as far away as possible. Tracy guessed this may have been their usual places for dinner. He turned to Adam first. "What can you tell me, Mr. Besserman, about the night your brother was killed?"

"I can tell you I didn't have anything to do with it. I was upstairs asleep in my bedroom. I retire early, and I sleep very sound."

Bebee nodded her head in agreement and rolled her eyes. "And my husband makes sounds like a runaway freight train."

Adam glared at his wife. "You know you are killing me, Bebee... if I end up dead someday, Detective, you will know where to look first. She's a no-holds-barred killer."

Tracy had to referee the two Bessermans quickly and get them back on track. "Okay, sir. You had nothing to do with the murder, but do you have any thoughts as to who might have? It would be someone here in the house that night. My boys have ruled out intruders. The windows were locked, and that trellis outside wouldn't hold more than twenty pounds, if that."

"Wow, Detective. You are asking me to point the finger at someone I know and live with. Probably a relative since the house is full of them. Well, you know what they say: relatives make the worst enemies."

"Did you hear anything about a note that was delivered that day by a Mr. Moore from the synagogue?"

"Yes. I heard it was something Aunt Marion wrote before she was conveniently swept overboard on The Bessie— that's the name of the Besserman yacht. I had nothing to do with Auntie's death; of course, I had nothing to gain. She never liked me for some reason, so Arnold was getting it all. And what I know about the note is that Arnie burned it before anyone else could read it, so you might want to question old Brenda Coleman. Or that fiancée of Lydia's, Paul Marx. In my opinion, they are both suspicious."

Adam Besserman looked past his wife, who had obviously ceased to exist in his eyes. "I'm sure you've already looked into my financial troubles, Detective. So I won't bother explaining my company's demise. I tried to salvage it." There was a loud guffaw out of Bebee Besserman at the end of the table as Adam continued. "I really did. I thought long and hard about doing something until I had convinced myself I had already done it. I tried to get Arnie to help me out, but he seemed to believe I would just be throwing good money after bad. Said he was trying to 'save' me from further headaches. What a joke that was."

After a few sundry questions of Bebee Besserman, Tracy dismissed the husband and wife, who exited the dining room by different doors that closed behind them with a slam.

Next, Tracy called Lydia Besserman's fiancée, Paul Marx, into the dining room. He soon found the twenty-six-year-old to be a very sensible young man. He was clean, nice-looking, and very straightforward, as well as being quick-witted and more than willing to help find who killed his fiancée's father. But in the end, he was of little help. He couldn't offer any new information or any reason that someone would want to kill Arnold Besserman. So Tracy moved on to another household guest, not normally in residence at the Besserman's.

Captain Brian Boyd entered the room and sat down in the nearest chair. He was a nice-enough-looking chap. Manning a yacht must be good for the body and soul, as Capt. Boyd seemed quite staunch and carried himself well inside a trim body with very little fat. He explained to Tracy that he had been staying in the house last night because Arnold had insisted. Mold had been found in the captain's house, and when Arnold heard, he told Sarina, the housemaid, to make up one of the spare bedrooms to house the captain overnight.

Like Lydia Besserman's fiancée before him, Captain Boyd couldn't offer much in the way of answers. He didn't know anything about the note. And he had no idea who would want to kill anyone in the Besserman family. Yes, he was on board the yacht the night Marion Besserman went over the starboard side, but in his estimation—and that of the Coast Guard—it was a clear

case of a terrible accident. And as far as Arnold
Besserman's murder went, he seemed truly at a loss for any
explanation. Tracy got the impression that the first
footprints on any empty beach would be Capt. Brian
Boyd's.

"Sorry I can't be of more help, Detective. You can't
harness the wind, but you can change your sails to get you
where you want to go. So let me know if you think of
anything I can do to adjust your rudder and change the
mainsail to help you get where you're headed."

Tracy smiled at the analogy. But he couldn't resist a
little cat-and-mouse questioning. "So, Captain. I have to
ask—didn't it bother you that she was married?"

Boyd looked slightly startled. But he didn't deny it.
"Perhaps you should ask if it bothered *her*, Detective."

Tracy didn't pursue the line of questioning.
Questionable fidelity was not on trial here, but it could be
the reason for murder. He thanked the captain and
dismissed him quickly; the man's use of nautical terms was
starting to annoy him. And he didn't want to waste any
time. All he needed to know about Aunt Marion's death
was probably in the statement taken by the Coast Guard
after her death. He could read that at a later time—but
doubted it would shed any light on his current predicament.
Or... maybe he was wrong.

When Tracy noticed the hour, he took some time
out from questioning the household. He wanted to get to
the local bookstore where Jamison McNalley was signing
books during the allotted time slot. He excused himself
with apologies to the people assembled and headed his car
uptown.

When he arrived, Mr. McNalley was being
altogether congenial with his fans. At a break in the action,
Tracy stepped up and asked for a private council in the
back of the store, over by the travel and leisure section.
There, amid picture books of faraway places with exotic

names, Tracy asked Arnold Besserman's fellow author if he had heard about the murder.

"Yes, I've heard, Detective. Arnold and I were not friends, but I am sorry to hear about his death. I know his wife Andrea must be beside herself. She is a delicate woman. High-strung."

"I understand you and Mr. Besserman had words recently over a charge of plagiarism. Is that correct?"

"Yes. That's correct. You must have heard that from Sally Myerson. She has a tendency to talk."

"What were the circumstances of the argument?"

"Nothing really. I asked him if he had taken his idea for *Forever and a Year* from my book, *The Year Long Day*. Said he didn't want to talk about it—immediately after making a rather boisterous denial."

"Did your argument get physical?"

"No. Of course not. We are not savages, and... are you leaning on me, Detective?"

"No. Well, maybe just a little. Now tell me... you don't believe Mr. Besserman was telling the truth?"

"No, Detective. The truth would have ended the conversation before it began."

"And you have no idea who would want to see Mr. Besserman dead?"

"No, of course not. He was a bag of wind who happened to get lucky with a few books. My guess is that Sally Myerson wrote most of the words you find on those pages. I tried to hire her once, but she is loyal to old Arnold."

Tracy thought for a moment. He was about to do a little bit of plagiarism himself. "If I may ask, sir... if this was fiction and you were writing the ending to this story, who would you come up with as the killer?"

McNalley thought for only a moment. "I don't write murder mysteries, Detective. I'm not clever enough. But, not the wife, of course—too obvious. And not the brother.

Once again, too obvious. Maybe not *any* members of the family. I think I would go with a member of the household staff. Arnold Besserman probably suffocated them. Maybe one of them snuck in, did the dastardly deed, and then snuck out. If he or she had gotten caught sneaking around in the house, it would be easily explained."

"Okay, Mr. McNalley. Here's my card in case you think of anything that might be helpful."

Jamison McNalley took the card and then stormed back to his book-signing table with one last look over his shoulder at Tracy, who was already moving through the bookstore and out the door to his car parked nearby. He was on a return trip to the Besserman house. He still had one more member of the household he needed to interrogate.

* * *

"Pretend to be poor. You'll notice a decrease in your friend list." —M.B. Johnson

The late Marion Besserman's nurse was gray-haired, short, stocky, and as starched as her white uniform. Her body stood ramrod straight and stiff as a cardboard cutout of herself. She would have made the perfect prison matron. Or inmate.

Tracy opened the questioning. "Thank you for joining me, Ms. Peters."

"You didn't say I had a choice, Detective."

Tracy took a deep breath. He needed to find a direct approach to this one. No back doors. "You are the late Marion Besserman's nurse, is that correct?"

"Yes."

"And yet you still reside in the Besserman home despite the fact that your charge has passed away."

"Yes. And if you must know, Detective, it is because they need me. Or did. Up until a few weeks ago, when Arnold gave me my walking papers along with a letter of recommendation. I have applied for an apartment in town, and I'm just waiting for approval from the landlord. Then I shall be moving out. Now, does that satisfy your curiosity?"

Yes, ma'am. Except, if you would please tell me how Ms. Marion Besserman died."

"Simple. She went up deck on *The Bessie* during a storm while I slept straight through, and she was swept overboard. At least, that was the Coast Guard's ruling. Accident, they said. But I'm not so sure."

"Do you have any basis for your suspicions?"

"No. Just my gut. Which is rarely wrong."

"Would it interest you to know that the coroner ruled Marion Besserman was dead before she hit the water? She did not drown. No water in the lungs. And now... do you think it's possible that someone killed Marion while she slept and before she was swept over? And if so, who do you suspect? And could it be the same person who killed Mr. Arnold Besserman?"

"Anything is possible, Detective. Maybe you should look to who stands to benefit the most from both of their deaths. Financially, Adam, of course, and his goofy wife. And Paul and Lydia can get married with her father out of the way. Arnold has been stonewalling that marriage for quite some time now. And of course, Arnold's wife Andrea gets a pretty nice chunk of change. She's having a fling with the captain of the yacht, you know. A girl's best friend is a near-sighted husband. And now with Arnold out of the way, they can carry on their shenanigans without worry. Those are just my observations, Detective. For whatever they are worth."

Tracy stopped making notes in his book and took a visible breath. "I'd say they are worth a great deal, Ms. Peters..."

"The people who know the least about you have the most to say." —Avliq L.

Tracy arrived on the synagogue steps the next morning at 8 a.m. He wasn't exactly sure what to expect. He had phoned ahead and asked for Mr. Delbert Moore to be available for questioning. The man on the other end of the line had grunted his consent and then hung up before Tracy could offer thanks. Was he going to receive a warm welcome or a chilly reception?

Could have gone either way. Luckily, it was the former. A man with a high hat and a long robe showed the detective into the main room and asked him to have a seat. Tracy complied with the request. He couldn't imagine anyone telling this ominous-looking man "no." It was several minutes before Mr. Delbert Moore appeared. He was dressed in some sort of gray-striped "work" jumpsuit and was carrying a large paint bucket. He set the bucket down before approaching Tracy for a good old-fashioned handshake. He possessed the demeanor of every janitor in every movie ever made.

"Hello, Detective. I've been expecting someone in authority to call on me. I guess you know I'm one of the last people to see Mr. Besserman alive. I hope his death wasn't the result of the envelope I delivered to him that morning. I would hate to think..."

"No, Mr. Moore. You did the right thing. Now, do you mind telling me exactly what transpired? How you came to find the envelope signed by Mrs. Marion Besserman."

"It's simple, really, Detective. I was straightening up the Tanakhs in the main hall here, and the envelope fell out. I saw it was signed by Marion... I knew her quite well up until her passing. I realized it might be important, so I delivered it to Mr. Besserman at the house. He's the next of kin. Mr. Besserman looked like he had seen a ghost."

"I guess in a way he had, Mr. Moore. At least a letter from a ghost. And that's it? You didn't tell anyone about the envelope. And you didn't open the envelope or read the letter inside?"

"No, sir. I would never do that. It wasn't any of my business."

"Okay. And who else was in the room when you gave Mr. Arnold Besserman the envelope?"

"Just Miss Myerson, his assistant. She's a nice lady."

"Other than Brooks, who let you in that morning, did you see or talk to anyone else?"

"No."

"How about back here at the synagogue? Did you tell anyone here about the envelope?"

"No. I didn't."

Tracy stood, thanked Delbert Moore, and made his way out of the synagogue. He could feel Mr. Moore's eyes watching him as he pushed open the door and stepped into the sunlight. His thoughts: *The letter was important.*

* * *

"There is no greater fall than from a burnt bridge." —C. Wallace

Tracy made a stop in the office of the Coast Guard. The boys there were very helpful. Cooperative. They supplied him with a report for the night that the aunt, Marion Besserman, was swept off the yacht during the violent storm. The report stated there was no indication that it was anything more than an accident. Mrs. Besserman was found floating in the water the next morning at first light.

Tracy interviewed the two seamen who filed the report. They said they had no reason to suspect foul play.

Everything seemed "above board." Really? It seemed more like "overboard" to a smart detective.

The next order of business sent Tracy back to look at the coroner's report. It was all there in black and white. Marion Besserman died of a heart attack. There was no water found in her lungs, which meant she was already dead when she hit the water. And there were no signs of trauma of any kind to the head or body. Natural causes were the only conclusion. If the family could be believed, she obviously went up on deck without their knowledge. Perhaps she was in the midst of a heart attack and became disoriented with pain, thinking she was going to someone's stateroom to get help. Then she took a wrong turn, ended up on deck, where she died. The storm could have swept her off the deck and into the ocean.

Next stop was Marion Besserman's regular physician. Dr. Wendal Assai informed Tracy that the woman had a bad ticker. That he had advised against travel, but she was a stubborn woman with her own mind. No dementia, just a bad heart and lungs. But she had become a bit paranoid in her later years. Paranoid? Tracy mulled over everything he had learned in the last few hours as he headed home; sunset was holding out until after 7, so there was still a hint of light as he turned onto his street. If the note was real, and Arnold didn't really kill his aunt, then why did she suspect that he would? Did someone put the idea in her head, knowing that she was suffering from paranoia? But why? What did they hope to gain? Maybe someone knew something. Did someone or something bring on the aunt's heart attack? Maybe Arnold Besserman knew what. Would the killer be out to silence him? Did the note bring out something in Arnold's memory? Or did it identify a killer?

* * *

*"Fake people are like fake jewelry. They look
great for a while and then they tarnish."*
—N. Prakash

Tracy had an appointment with the Besserman
lawyer at 10 the next morning. He went straight from the
precinct, traveling uptown, to the law firm of Hutchins,
Grover and Moss. His appointment was with Mr. Moss, a
small, bespectacled, Lionel Barrymore-looking man
wearing a pinstriped suit and a yellow tie, who received
him with a cordial handshake and an offer of coffee. Tracy
accepted both.

"The parties concerned already know what they are
inheriting, Detective. Mr. Arnold Besserman insisted on
having a meeting after his Aunt Marion died and her wealth
was distributed. Arnold received the bulk of her estate. So
he, in turn, made the terms of his own will known as
everyone sat in this very room. He laid out the plan, his
wishes. I advised against such a thing, but my words fell on
deaf ears. So, everyone knows exactly what they are
getting. Maybe you just want to confirm that everyone is
telling the truth?"

Tracy was actually thinking "no," but he said, "Yes,
Mr. Moss. Something like that."

Moss pulled out a paper from his drawer, cleaned
his glasses with the edge of his sleeve, and then began to
read at lightning speed. "The wife, Andrea Besserman, will
receive $5 million. Same for the daughter, Lydia
Besserman. Mr. Besserman's brother, Adam, will receive
$1 million. Salley Myerson receives $1 mil. Brooks
Johnson, $500k. The household cook, Chilly Rodriguez,
and the maid, Sarina Medina, $100k each. Brenda Peters,
the late Marion Besserman's nurse, $10k. And the captain
of The Bessie, the family yacht, will receive $10k. And
there is a small trust fund set up for the continuation of the

book writing. Miss Sally Myerson will be executor of that phase. She will finish Mr. Besserman's unfinished works and take charge of the handling with the publishers, etc. And that's about it. Mrs. Besserman and her daughter, of course, get the house, The Bessie, and the contents of both." Mr. Moss stopped and peered over the top of his glasses. The look on his face said, "Get ready for this one." Tracy braced himself. "…And all of this is going to go off just as I have read it to you, Detective, because Mr. Arnold Besserman never got a chance to make a couple of changes to his will. Would you like to know what those changes were going to be?"

* * *

Armed with the latest information, that afternoon Tracy stopped in at the Besserman house. He asked everyone to assemble in the study. And they did. Tracy observed everyone, without seeming to do so. And then he began his summation even before the last person could find their seat.

"Okay, folks, this is what I have. Everyone in this room is considered a suspect. Until cleared. And so far, I have not cleared anyone. You all claim to be elsewhere in the house the night of the murder, but there was an outline on the shade with Arnold Besserman. So someone or everyone is telling a lie. Because the outline on the shade that Lydia and Ms. Myerson saw from the driveway could have been either a man or a woman, and in both of their statements they said that the assailant was approximately the same size as Arnold, who was 5'9" according to the autopsy report, I have a dilemma. Every one of you is about the same height. And that includes you, Captain Boyd, and you, Brooks. In addition, the forensic report has come back. No prints were found here in the study except for Arnold's and Miss Myerson's. No prints on the murder weapon—the

87

poker was wiped clean. The only thing we know for certain is that Arnold Besserman died from blunt instrument trauma. Today's answers to tomorrow's questions: nothing. Anywhere. Another dead end. I will be back when I have some answers."

Tracy dismissed everyone and headed to the front door.

* * *

*"Fake friends get mad when we pretend
to like them." —C. Wallace*

Tracy sat down with his cousin for a nice, leisurely dinner at The Blue Water Grill. He wasn't going to bring up his latest case unless Tony asked. But of course he did. Tony fancied himself a first-class sleuth. Tracy swore him to secrecy and then laid out the suspects in the case with as much detail as he could. When he was done, Tony sat back and stared into his plate of salmon.

"What about a description of all these 5'9" suspects… physically? Sometimes you tell me that is a dead giveaway. Or have you abandoned all your usual methods on this one?"

"Nothing really outstanding. Daughter is very gothic, anti-establishment. Wife is a fashion plate, everything perfect. Assistant is mousy, walks with a limp, sometimes a cane. The younger brother is a non-descript man. Wears a toupee. His wife is like a chameleon—she blends into the wall. The captain of the yacht is a burly man, former military, I am guessing. The nurse is a prison matron in sweaters and long skirts. And the houseman could have played Cheeves the butler in any English movie."

"Okay, let's go back to the women. Wife is impeccable, brother's wife is nondescript, daughter is out there, the assistant is mousy, walks with a limp. By the way, a limp? Is it a recent injury?”

“I don’t know. I never wanted to ask.”

“Well, maybe you should. But don’t ask her directly. Call the houseman. He will give you all the scoop. My guess is that he knows everything about everyone in the house.”

Tracy agreed. He addressed his cousin once more. “Okay, so what about the rest? Now that you have heard the details, what do you think?”

“I think, Detective, that you need to recreate the crime. Someone is lying to you.”

“Well, to tell you the truth, I didn’t think I needed to. I have the girls downstairs looking up at the shade. I have all the suspects somewhere else in the house. I have the houseman Brooks downstairs. He goes to answer the door when the girls knock…”

“Which means the door was locked. And why was the front door locked?”

“Maybe it was always locked at that hour. It was late. The daughter was taking the assistant home, and she could use her key to get in when she got back.”

“Then why *didn’t* she use her key? Why did she have to call for the houseman to let them in?”

Tracy thought for a moment. Brooks was the one who sent the two women out of the room, saying he would check Mr. Besserman, stay with him until the police arrived. *Was Besserman really dead? Did the butler make sure he was dead? He was the last person alone with Besserman. And he let the women in that night.*

“Maybe she knocked because she was in a panic. Maybe she thought it was faster to call the houseman. Maybe I’ve overlooked something…”

* * *

*"When you see genuine, you
give up dealing with the fake." —N. Davani*

Tracy was back in the Besserman house. He was taking Tony's advice. He had asked the two women, Sally and Lydia, to go down to the front porch where they were the night of the murder. Next, he had Brooks go into the kitchen with the cook and the maid. Then, on his signal, Lydia and Sally knocked real hard on the front door. Tracy waited in the kitchen with Brooks to see if it was possible to hear the knocking from the kitchen. It wasn't.

Brooks began to explain he must have been mistaken about where he was, exactly. Tracy silenced him with a raised hand. He then started walking closer to the front door. There was no sound until he got to the foot of the stairs. He now knew there was no way Brooks could have heard the women knocking from the kitchen. Brooks had to be in the front of the house, not the back… near the staircase. *Why did he lie?*

Tracy then went up the steps as the women continued to knock. He tried the study… the sound traveled up the staircase. It was clear. He then went to each room with an occupant that night. The sound was clear in Adam and Bebee Besserman's rooms. The sound was clear in Andrea Besserman's room. But the sound was greatly diminished by the time you got to the guest bedroom where Captain Boyd was sleeping. And even more diminished in Brenda Cook's bedroom. The starched nurse would have heard nothing. Tracy was suddenly questioning his assessment of Brooks.

Why did he lock the front door that night after the women had gone? He couldn't have heard the women knocking when they came back. He was the last person in the room with Arnold Besserman before the police came. Was Jamison McNalley, the rival author, right about the ending to this story? Was it possible that Brooks killed his employer? Why? Money? Tracy had already looked into Brooks Johnson's past, and there were no skeletons. And he had no current financial woes, other than taking care of his invalid mother. So why the need for money?

Tracy came back down the stairs and opened the front door so the women could stop pounding (the noise was giving him a headache). He then thanked everyone and took his leave. He needed answers. This was a bend in the road. But a bend is only the end of the road if you don't make the turn.

* * *

Now convinced that Brooks had something to do with the murder of Arnold Besserman, the next morning Tracy stopped back at the mansion to see the houseman. But Brooks was not there. He was out. While waiting for the butler's return, Tracy questioned Sarina the maid and Chilly the cook. They both recalled that Brooks was in the kitchen with them the night of the murder. However, they didn't remember hearing the pounding on the door. All they remembered was Brooks leaving the kitchen, and when they went to investigate, they saw Lydia Besserman and Sally Myerson running up the stairs. Brooks told them both to go back to the kitchen. And they did. Tracy made a few notes in his book and then told both women he would be back later and to please ask Brooks to remain at the house when he returned from his errands.

As he was leaving, Tracy passed Lydia Besserman in the foyer. She was decapitating tulips in a vase on the table, her mind a million miles away. She barely noticed him. "Hello, Lydia. Are you okay?"

"Oh, Detective Tracy… yes, I'm fine… I guess. I was just thinking about Daddy and how he always told me to be a good daughter. But he never told me how. I am great at being a rebel. It's the rest of my life that I suck at."

"Don't be so hard on yourself. You are going to be okay. Just take some time to grieve. Grief demands answers, but sometimes there are none." *(He had heard that somewhere. Sound advice.)* "Maybe if you help me solve this murder, it will give you some peace. If you don't mind, I have a few questions about that night. Do you think you are up to answering them?"

Lydia put the shears down on the foyer table. Her hair was droopier than normal, her face paler. But her eyes seemed to focus back into the present. She nodded her consent.

"Okay, was it usual for the front door to be locked at a certain time?"

"No set time."

"Okay. And how far down the driveway was the car that night?"

Lydia grabbed for Tracy's hand and led him out the front door and down the steps. She stopped about twenty yards down the horseshoe drive. "Here, Detective."

Tracy looked back at the study window. Even at night, the two women would be able to see the window clearly, along with any outlines on the shade. Tracy then asked the young woman something he had never asked her before. "In your opinion… was the person hitting your father a man or a woman?"

Lydia thought for a moment and then turned to Tracy with a look of bewilderment. "It happened so fast, Detective. I mean, my first thought… 'this is a dream.' Second thought… 'no it isn't.' Third thought… 'oh crap.'"

"Then why don't you describe to me exactly what it was you saw."

"I don't know, Detective. To be honest, it was difficult to see— *really* see—but then when we got to the study, there Daddy was, on the floor."

Tracy nodded. He was starting to get the picture. *Maybe he had been right all along. When your gut says one thing and your head says another… your head loses.*

* * *

"The future allows the past to make perfect sense." —Anonymous

Sally Myerson unlocked the front door with her key and stepped inside the Besserman house. She called out a greeting, and when there was no sign of anyone, she climbed the stairs and went straight to the study/office to begin work on her current manuscript. She would catch up with the rest of the family before lunch. She unlocked the study door with the key in the hall table and then entered the room. She leaned her cane against the wall and started toward the desk. From behind her back there came a nice, friendly greeting. "Good morning."

Sally Myerson jumped a mile, then sat down hard in a nearby chair. "Oh, you startled me, Detective. What are you doing here so early?"

"I'm here to confront a killer."

"Really? You mean you know who killed Arnold? Or is it Aunt Marion's killer you want to confront?"

"I'm standing by the Coast Guard ruling, Ms. Myerson. Marion Besserman had a heart attack and, undoubtedly, during the seizure, she took a wrong turn out of her cabin and ended up on the deck where she died and was eventually swept into the water. There was no evidence of foul play."

"But what about the note in the synagogue? Why did Marion think Arnold was going to kill her?"

"Marion Besserman was getting a bit paranoid in her old age. Everyone knew it. So someone planted that seed in her mind. Or… a person in this house faked that note, hoping that someone would find it and Arnold would be investigated."

"Really, Detective… I don't know."

Tracy pulled out a chair. "Yes, you do, Ms. Myerson. Please sit down. Two people know that you have been lying, and they are both in this room."

Sally Myerson did as she was told. Slowly, methodically, she lowered herself into the seat.

"Here's what happened the night Mr. Arnold Besserman died. Tell me if I'm right. You killed Mr. Besserman by striking him on the head with the fire poker. You wiped the poker clean and laid it beside him. You then left the room, locking the door behind you. Next, you went downstairs to where Lydia was waiting beside her car. When you got into the car, you changed your mind about riding with her, for some reason…"

"She's a very bad driver, Detective. I fear for my life."

"…so instead of waiting for someone to find Arnold later, you suddenly got the idea to pretend to look back and see someone in the window. Perfect. You couldn't be the killer if you saw the murder from the driveway. And you were so convincing that Lydia actually believed she saw someone too. But later, she realized she was only taking your word."

"That's absurd but go on with your story."

"Both you and Lydia ran back to the house, where Brooks let you in, and then you all discovered the body together. You gave yourself and Lydia the perfect alibi. Well, almost perfect. And it would have worked too, if I hadn't asked Lydia a few questions about the killer on the shade."

"You have no evidence that points to me. You said yourself there were no fingerprints on the poker. And why would I kill my golden goose? Arnold was paying me to basically ghostwrite for him. So why would I want to kill him?"

"Because I found out from Arnold Besserman's attorney that he was getting ready to sign some papers that would have cut you out of his will. Cut you right out of those million dollars."

"Really?"

"Yes. And you knew it. He had discovered the little fling between his wife and the yacht captain, Brian Boyd, so he called his attorney, Mr. Moss, and said he was changing his will to eliminate the captain's inheritance. And for whatever reason, he was cutting you out as well. And knowing as much as you did about everything that Mr. Besserman did, I'm sure you found out somehow or overheard his phone call. The law firm had the papers ready, so you had to kill him before he could sign."

"Yes, I knew he was taking me out of the will. So what? He said I was getting greedy. He had been paying me to write for him, but he had also been paying me on the side ever since the accident."

"You mean the accident with you in the front seat? I asked Brooks why you limped, why you needed to use that cane, and he told me all about it."

"Yes, Detective. Arnold was as bad a driver as his daughter. He was driving me home one night and he hit a tree. He had been drinking, even though he didn't want to admit it. I was badly injured. I have been walking with a cane ever since. He paid me to keep me from suing him. He said he would compensate me and then put me in the will for a million. He also promised that when he retired he would get his publishers to give me a shot at my own books. With my name and my picture on the jacket."

"So what happened? Why did he change his mind about all that he promised you?"

"I don't know. He just woke up one day and decided I was getting too much. The extra payment every month on top of my salary was just extravagant, he said. He called me greedy. What a laugh. I was doing all the work and he was getting all the credit. Who was really the greedy one?"

"So he would continue to pay you, but you wouldn't get the inheritance?"

"Yes. And I was counting on that million. I had tolerated Arnold for years, just to get that money. When I complained, he would tell me: 'If you want rainbows, Sally old girl… then you have to put up with the rain.'"

"So, now you were going to continue to submit his work, using your name and his, hoping the publishers take the work posthumously? Is that the plan?"

"Yes. Something like that. There are even a couple of movie people sniffing around. Might be an option for a film in the works. But there are no shortcuts to any place worth going, Detective. I have to be the one to finish what we started."

"Can you do all this from prison, Ms. Myerson? Because that's where you are going."

"Oh come, Detective. You have no evidence. You have no one to dispute my eyewitness to the crime, other than Lydia. Who puts stock in what she says? She is distraught. Suffering from depression. I'm sure with half a chance I can convince her again that she saw something on that shade. So, you have nothing, really."

Sally Myerson limped across the room to her writing desk and opened her purse. She removed some cosmetics and a small compact with a mirror and began to apply some makeup as she spoke. "…And the reason you have nothing is because I have been making this up as we went along. I didn't kill Arnold. I was just writing a story, giving you a little demonstration of what I do best. You were just like Arnold, feeding me an idea and then asking me to run with it." The assistant snapped the compact closed after examining her handiwork. "Sorry, Detective, but I couldn't resist."

"Okay, Ms. Myerson. Then tell me this. Did Marion Besserman really write the note that Delbert Moore found?"

"I don't know, Detective. But I do know who burned that note in the fireplace. I did. Before anyone—like snoopy old Brooks out there—could see it."

Tracy stood up and walked to the fireplace. He turned back to see a smile on Sally Myerson's face. She had removed her glasses, fluffed up her hair a bit. A new woman was emerging from her cocoon. The detective closed his notebook, returned it to his jacket, and started for the door. "I'm walking out of here without an admission of guilt, Miss Myerson, and I take it you are going to let me. But I will find a way to make a conviction stick. It may take a while, but I'm patient. So stay on your toes."

"Touché, Detective. Don't worry, I will. The slender reed may bend in the face of the strong winds, but it will stand tall when the storm has passed."

Without another word, Tracy left the room where Arnold Besserman was murdered in cold blood. Brooks showed him to the front, shook his hand, and then closed the door behind him. It would be years before anyone would even attempt to reopen the cold case file marked *Arnold Besserman Homicide*—and even then there was no way to charge Sally Myerson with first-degree murder. Miss Myerson would move to Paris, where she was soon languishing in fame on the banks of the Seine. And…

Every Valentine's Day, Detective Tracy received a copy of Sally Myerson's latest bestselling novel—and a card containing a recent snapshot of the now world-famous author. At the bottom of each card was one word: *Touché.* Guess that would be a double *touché*, Detective Tracy.

MURDERS HAPPEN EVERYDAY

PROLOGUE

The old apartment house on the Upper East Side of Manhattan had never seen a murder. Or a murder investigation. Even though it had undoubtedly seen just about everything else in its 100-year history. To New York City homicide detective Nick Tracy, these facts didn't make a whole lot of difference. When he walked into the pre-war building, he found the structure was loaded with character and possessed an "old soul," reflected in loose floorboards and rattling windowpanes. The doorman's greeting suggested to Tracy that the tall, thin man with the epaulets on his jacket was enjoying all the excitement a bit too much; he seemed to blurt out the first thing that came to mind when he was shown Tracy's gold shield.

"Hey, Detective. Got us a murder here in the old building. You coming to investigate? Thought you might be. Up on the third floor, apartment 3-D. Nice man, Mr. Montgomery. You won't find much, I can tell you that. There's no evidence. No suspects. No nothin'. It's a real mystery who done this one. I wouldn't want to be in your shoes, no sir."

After thanking the doorman for his unsolicited take on the crime, Tracy walked across the lobby and took the elevator up to the third floor and the apartment with the bright yellow crime tape crisscrossing the doorway. He removed the tape, stepped over the threshold, and into a case with such a surprise conclusion that even a seasoned officer like Tracy could never have predicted that unusual piece of evidence that would seal the killer's fate.

* * *

"Feminism is the radical notion that women are people."—Marie Shear

Detective Tracy took a good look around the apartment, which had been remodeled to bring it into the 1970s. The foyer was wider than most and was lined on both sides with matching drop-leaf tables, holding vases of real cut flowers. Nice touch.

Once in the front room, the first thing Tracy did was to greet his men, listen to their take on the evidence, and then examine the position of the body; in this case, the dead man was still in a sitting position in an easy chair, slumped over, with a gaping wound on the back of his head. The chair was facing the console television, which was still playing. (J.R. and Bobby Ewing were getting their final licks in with Cliff Barnes.) Tracy walked over, pushed the off button, and watched for a moment as *Dallas* faded to black.

When he turned to his left, he noticed there was a dining table with dirty dishes and remnants of an earlier meal: four plates, four glasses, and various utensils. On a small occasional table near a large credenza, the murder weapon was resting—a heavy iron statue that had been tagged and bagged. Tracy could see traces of hair and human tissue through the clear plastic wrapping but was guessing that the statue would be wiped clean of the killer's prints. Perps today were developing skills far superior to their predecessors.

The responding officer, Patrolman Stone, had detained several women and separated them into three different rooms. He informed Tracy that the three consisted of: 1) the woman who found the body, 2) the next-door neighbor who witnessed the discovery, and 3) the neighbor across the hall who witnessed the witness making the discovery.

After imparting a few details regarding the case, Stone left Tracy to follow through. Tracy made the decision to start with the woman who had found the body, Rose Thorne—the live-in girlfriend of the victim. It was the perfect place to start.

Stepping through the kitchen door, Tracy found a woman standing at the sink with her back his way. The latest Neil Diamond song was playing on a tape at her elbow. She was a tall, reedy woman with red hair that fell softly to her shoulders. He could see she was wearing a pantsuit that hugged her curves in a good way; mannish but feminine. When she turned, Tracy was stunned by her beauty. He was taken back for a moment but recovered nicely. "I'm Detective Tracy, Miss Thorne. I understand you found Mr. Montgomery when you returned…" Tracy quickly consulted the notes he had taken during the discussion with Patrolman Stone. "…that was shortly after ten?"

"Yes, Detective. Randolph and I live here. In unwedded bliss. I arrived home maybe 10:15."

"And you left the home at what time?"

"Approximately 8:30. We had guests for dinner. When I left, Randolph's niece and her husband were still here. I don't know what time they departed."

"I'm going to need their phone number… and by the way, where did you go during the time you left the apartment and your return at 10:15? And did anyone see you?"

Rose Thorne smiled for the first time. "Yes. A lot of people saw me, Detective. I was the speaker at a women's rights rally. I can give you the exact location if you need it."

Tracy eyed the blood on the woman's trousers and fingers. His thought: *I'm going to require a lot more than that, lady… and why in the world haven't you washed your hands.* Out loud he said, "I will need all of the particulars, Miss Thorne… and now can you tell me what you found when you entered the apartment? Please don't leave out any details—they may be important."

"I see, Detective. The truth, the whole truth, and nothing but the truth—is that it?"

"Yes."

"Okay. I entered the apartment and found Randolph in his seat. The television was still on. Randolph was quite an avid television watcher and he doesn't usually leave that ratty old chair when his programs are showing. From what I could see, it appeared he had been struck in the back of the head. It was awful. I touched him to see if he was breathing—he wasn't—and then I picked up the phone and called for an ambulance and the police." It sounded like a well-rehearsed speech.

"Is there anything else, Miss Thorne?"

"No."

"And have you spoken with the niece and her husband yet? To determine exactly what time they left?"

"No, I have not. Should I? I thought that was some policeman's job."

"You're right, Miss Thorne. I will ask them myself. If you will please write down their phone number and address for me. And sometime in the near future I will need you to come down to the station for a formal statement. I will let you know when."

Tracy watched as Rose Thorne went to a desk and wrote down some numbers and then returned to his side. She smelled like Angel perfume. He noticed that the edge of the paper held a smear of blood. He also noticed, as she handed him the paper, there wasn't a tear or a sniffle coming from the cool feminist. *You are strong, you are invincible… you are woman… huh, Ms. Thorne?*

* * *

"Girls just want to have FUNdamental rights."
— Cyndi Lauper

Tracy left Rose Thorne and moved to the back of the apartment. The second woman his man had detained was waiting for him in the master bedroom. She jumped to her feet when she noticed Tracy had entered the room. She was a short, middle-aged woman with bobbed hair that was turning silver. She wore horn-rimmed glasses that slid down to the tip of her nose. In contrast to Rose Thorne, she was dressed as the proverbial housewife with nowhere to go outside her own apartment.

"Thank God you're here. I've been waiting and waiting. And with poor Randolph's body just in the next room. I don't think I'll be able to sleep tonight. And I'm not going back in there until you take that woman away. You *have* arrested her, haven't you?"

Tracy took a breath. He knew the type. "I assume you are speaking of Miss Thorne. I have just spoken with her and—"

"Of course I'm speaking of Miss Thorne. Who else? She killed him. There's no doubt."

"What makes you so sure, Miss…?"

"Radcliff. Mabel Radcliff. And what do you mean, what makes me so sure? Of course I'm sure. Who wouldn't be? I walked in and found her standing over his chair holding the iron statue in her hand. It was his favorite piece. He brought it back from Korea—got it during the war. And *she* killed him with it. She is cold-hearted, that one."

"But you didn't actually see Miss Thorne strike Mr. Montgomery?"

"Well, no. I didn't need to. She was standing there, holding the weapon, with blood on her hands and clothes… what more do you want? Polaroids? And by the way, it's *Mrs.*, Detective. My husband and I have been neighbors of Randolph's for ten years. He moved in with his wife, Muriel, and then she died about two years later. We have been his friends as well as his neighbors. It's an old building. The walls are thin, and we are right next door. Albert and I hear things."

"You mean there were loud arguments between Mr. Montgomery and Miss Thorne?"

"Sometimes. But she doesn't raise her voice much. She's a cool customer. Feminist, you know."

"Okay, Mrs. Radcliff. If we need a statement from you, I will contact you and bring you down to the station. Here's my card. If you think of anything that might be helpful in the way of concrete evidence, please let me know. Thank you for your assistance."

Mabel Radcliff took the card. She read it over and then turned to Tracy as he left the room. "She did it, Detective Tracy. I know you think I'm just an old busybody… but I know she did it. If she gets away with this, there will have been *two* crimes committed here."

* * *

"…Just try dismissing half the planet."
— Anonymous feminist

The third woman who had been detained was waiting in the study. She was a woman of medium height, medium build, with blonde hair pulled up on top of her head in a neat little knot. She appeared to be about the age of Miss Thorne—somewhere in her early 40s. She wasn't glamorous like Rose Thorne, just pretty in a natural way. Her face was void of makeup—not even lipstick—and she was dressed in jeans and a plain white sweater. Of course, it may have been a $700 sweater for all Tracy knew. She smiled when Tracy entered the room and slowly held out her hand. "I'm Deb Ross. I live across the hall… 3G. And I assume you are Detective Tracy. The nice police officer said you would be coming in to question me. What can I do to help?"

Tracy shook the outstretched hand and then released it. He liked Deb Ross instantly. "Did you hear or see anything, Miss Ross? Mr. Montgomery was killed sometime after 8:30 and before 10:15. And do you have any idea who might have a reason to kill the man?"

"I didn't hear anything, no. Other than Randolph's TV—he turns it up so loud because his hearing is gone. And I was home all night. Alone. But I did speak to several people on the phone during those hours, in case you want to check. I can supply you with the names and numbers. And as far as knowing someone who would want to kill Randolph… I think it's fairly obvious, Detective, don't you?"

"No, I don't, Miss Ross. If you are referring to Miss Thorne, she was speaking at a rally uptown tonight."

"Oh? That does change things, doesn't it? At first I thought maybe Randolph had a heart attack. President Carter let that Patty Hearst out of prison recently, and Jimmy Carter is not one of Randolph's favorite people. Thinks the man is going to ruin the country. But then when I found out Randolph was murdered, I guess I just assumed Rose would be the number one suspect, being the girlfriend and all. And from what I know…"

"And that is?"

"I don't want to say, Detective, because it's mainly just intuition—woman's intuition—but I don't trust her. I know she is a feminist and a big supporter of women's rights, which I agree with. But she didn't love Randolph. I wanted something better for him. He was a really nice man. After his wife died, he went through a rough patch. He dated a few of his late wife's friends. And then he met Rose. He kind of fell for her. When she moved in, I had a bad feeling—like she was just using him for an address. But then they seemed to get along so well. Despite what Mabel Radcliff says, they didn't fight that often."

"What about the niece and her husband? Were they in the habit of visiting often?"

"Yes. They like to stay close to their future money. I am sure they are shopping for a better house as we speak. They knew they were Randolph's only heirs. And now, if you are going to ask me if they are capable of murder… I would have to say 'maybe.' I don't think I need to tell you, Detective, that you never know what's in someone's heart. Murder happens every day."

* * *

"Men of quality do not fear equality."
— Anonymous

It was the morning after the murder of Randolph Montgomery. Tracy's knock was answered by a short young woman, somewhere in her early thirties, with mousy brown hair and a pale complexion. Linda Montgomery Beecher stepped aside to let Tracy pass and then led the way into a modest living room with old-fashioned and overstuffed furniture—hand-me-downs from generous relatives, no doubt.

"I'm so glad you came, Detective. I am hoping you have arrested that Thorne woman for the murder of my uncle. He was such a dear. And I'm sure you want to know... we left my uncle's apartment at 8:45."

"No. I have not arrested Miss Thorne. You of all people must know that Rose Thorne was speaking at a rally during the time your uncle was killed. She says she got up from the dinner table at 8:30."

"So what, Detective? The next-door neighbor, Mabel Radcliff, called and said she saw her standing over the chair with the murder weapon in her hand. She had blood on her clothes. What are you looking for here, a confession? Because you are not going to get one. Rose will never admit to anything; she will declare her innocence all the way to the firing squad."

"I understand how you feel, Mrs. Beecher. And I have considered the possibility that Miss Thorne killed your uncle. I am waiting for word from the coroner. Maybe he can place the time of death closer to 10. There are a lot of fingers pointing her way. But I need substantial evidence, not just a bunch of people who think it's her... or who want it to be her. The law doesn't work that way. There needs to be tangible proof to convict."

"I understand, Detective. I have great faith... you will find something. Because if she didn't do it, I can't think of a soul alive who would."

Tracy glanced around the room. "Where is Mr. Beecher? Will he be joining us?"

"Oh, didn't I tell you? Harry had to go into our shop today. Business matters."

Tracy didn't feel like traipsing around town looking for Harry Beecher, who was obviously avoiding him. He wanted to follow up with Rose Thorne. She was staying with a friend until forensics was complete, and she could have the apartment cleaned—maybe of all traces of Randolph Montgomery. "Okay. Thanks, Mrs. Beecher. I need the name and number of your uncle's lawyer, and then I will see myself out. Here's my card in case you think of something important to this case. I'm going to need your cooperation and that of your husband. I may be back soon, or I may call you into the station for some more questions."

With the name of James Osgood, attorney at law, Tracy left the Beecher house and headed to a pay phone. He called the Chief and told him he was going to ask Rose Thorne to come to the precinct right away for some serious questioning. He then headed to the precinct himself. He would check with his medical examiner as to time of death. Everyone was pointing a finger her way, and everyone couldn't be wrong. Or could they?

* * *

"No mothers? No founding fathers!"
— Anonymous

The interrogation room had been empty when Rose Thorne arrived. She now sat with her feet beneath the table, her hands folded in front of her like a schoolgirl—the picture of innocence. It was Tracy that paced back and forth, stopping on occasion to make a point. "Look, Miss Thorne, my coroner can't fix the time of death of Randolph Montgomery any closer than between 8:30 and 10:00. And that's bad news for you. You had more than enough time to deliver your speech, get back in the cab, and return home to kill Mr. Montgomery and call the police. You were found holding the murder weapon. Yours are the only prints on the weapon. The blows to the head with the blunt instrument killed Mr. Montgomery almost instantly. And the time element is not your friend here, Miss Thorne. And everyone I talked to has said…"

"That I did it... I can understand that, Detective. But have you spoken with the rally people? Ms. Rawlings and her group? They can vouch for my time there. Or you could just call all the two hundred women in the audience." A

107

slight smile played at the corner of Rose Thorne's mouth. Tracy didn't like being toyed with

"This is a very serious situation, Miss Thorne. I wouldn't make light of anything in this case."

The slight smile turned downward. Rose Thorne's head whipped back in defiance. "I'm not making light of anything, Detective. I am asking you to please go and see Ms. Rawlings. She is the head of the committee. She is the one who hired me to speak—if you can call it speaking... actually, I'm very good at making something that, at its core, is very uninteresting... seem interesting." Rose Thorne seemed to shake off her thoughts and then jump back on track. "...Ms. Rawlings can tell you everything, Detective. Please go and see her. If I can smoke, I will remain here in this room until you get back."

Tracy knocked on the door of the interrogation room, a signal to let him out. Two precinct clerks took his place in the room. He informed them Miss Thorne would be remaining there. Rose Thorne smiled at both of the men like a schoolgirl. Tracy didn't like the gesture. He thought Thorne was still making light of the situation. He addressed his number one suspect. "Okay. I'm going. I'll call the number and let them know I'm on the way. And you had better hope that this Ms. Rawlings has a real good memory and 20/20 eyesight, or I'll be back here to read you your rights. Everyone who comes into this room thinks they can have their way with my team. But right after they believe they have the upper hand—and just before they are booked... they end up staring at ME."

With that, Tracy left the room. He banged open the precinct door angrily, almost shattering the glass on his way out.

"Make it a feminist world..."
— Marilyn French

Tracy arrived at the lecture hall in record time. He would have gotten a speeding ticket if he hadn't been a cop. He found Mrs. Rawlings waiting patiently for his arrival. She was a stout woman with bookish glasses and the refined air of a schoolteacher. She escorted Tracy to the back room, where a young man awaited their entrance. He was an exact masculine replica of Mrs. Rawlings. And he was standing beside the latest in 1979 recording devices.

"This is my son Eric, Detective Tracy. He conducts all the recordings for our lectures. He is quite talented. We try to record whatever we can, for posterity. Someday we will look back and remember when. Too bad our forefathers didn't have these devices. How wonderful it would be if we could watch over their shoulders."

Before Tracy could comment, as if on cue, Eric Rawlings pushed the start button, and the image of Rose Thorne appeared on the small screen in front of them. It was her test run. There was a timer at the bottom of the recording showing the time: 9:07 p.m. Tracy watched as the next recording came into view. It was the image of Rose Thorne taking the stage, standing at the podium and beginning her speech—9:20 p.m. Eric Rawlings fast-forwarded through the speech to the end, as Rose Thorne left the stage amid a huge round of applause and a standing ovation. 9:48 p.m.

The Rawlings both turned to Tracy. They looked very pleased with themselves. Tracy was pleased too. "Thank you both for your cooperation. I will show myself out."

* * *

Tracy's next stop on the way back to the precinct was the law firm of Campbell and Osgood. Mr. James Osgood himself received Tracy with a big smile and a handshake before getting down to the serious business of who benefited from the death of Randolph Montgomery. The legal wheels were in motion, so there was no worry of breaching client privilege. Mr. Osgood was able to speak somewhat freely.

"Benefiting from Randolph's will, huh... of course, there's the Beechers. They are to inherit a nice little sum. It will no doubt help. Linda accompanied Randolph a couple of weeks ago when he came in to sign the codicil we drew up for him."

"You say, a few weeks ago?"

"Yes. He hadn't updated his will since his wife died. He wanted to make some drastic changes to fit his life, now that Muriel was gone."

"And I'm assuming that Rose Thorne benefited as well."

"Yes, Detective. She would benefit a great deal... but if she killed him, well... too bad. Even though the codicil leaves the money for her work with the feminist movement, she would have complete control. She could have paid herself any amount she wanted for management fees and such. As it stands right now, the foundation which she controls gets 50% of Randolph's money. She gets the apartment free and clear. The Beechers get 40%."

"And what about the remaining 10%?"

James Osgood consulted the papers in front of him. "Oh yes. Some goes to various charities, and some goes to the widow across the hallway, Deborah Ross. Randolph liked her. They were good friends, and he knew she was going to run out of her late husband's insurance money sometime in the near future. Randolph Montgomery was a

110

very generous and caring man, Detective. That is why this murder is so disturbing. I have been to that apartment so many times in the past years. And now I can't get that imaginative picture out of my mind... Randolph sitting in that chair of his, covered in blood with his skull bashed in. I am hoping that you have Miss Thorne in custody. I would hate to see her get away with it."

"Whether in custody or not, Mr. Osgood, I'm not sure if a good lawyer couldn't get her off on circumstantial evidence... which makes me ask, why are you so sure she is guilty?"

James Osgood leaned back in his leather chair, looking shocked. "Why, I just assumed she did it, Detective. She certainly had the motive and opportunity. And like they always say—'look at the wife or girlfriend first.' Maybe assumptions are premature here."

"See, Mr. Osgood, Rose Thorne has an alibi for the night in question. I hope I can find out who actually killed Mr. Montgomery... because I'm not sure that Rose Thorne did it."

* * *

Back at the precinct, Tracy spoke first. His detainee's composure was still intact. "I'm sorry, Miss Thorne, but I'm holding you now for the murder of Randolph Montgomery. You had a motive: money. Montgomery's will benefited you above all others. And you had the opportunity: you arrived home in plenty of time to commit the murder before Mabel Radcliff showed up on your doorstep. It would have been easy if Mr. Montgomery were asleep in the chair when you walked through that door. You came off the stage at 9:48, and it's a fifteen-minute cab ride from the hall where you spoke back to your apartment. Plenty of time. Mabel saw you standing over the body with the murder weapon in your hand and blood on your clothes. It's a smoking gun eyewitness account."

"You are making a dreadful mistake, Detective Tracy. I didn't do this horrible thing."

"You must know, Miss Thorne, that everyone who has ever sat in that chair has said that very thing."

"I'm sure they have... but I'm not everyone. I'm somebody. *I am woman, hear me roar.* I'm sure you know the words, Detective."

Tracy felt like he was locking eyes with a mama lion. The look in Rose Thorne's eyes was fierce. "Then you are admitting that your alibi might not hold up in court, Miss Thorne?"

"Then you are admitting that I have one, Detective?"

Without looking back, Tracy left the room. Rose Thorne would be read her rights and allowed a phone call to her attorney. The lawyer might have her out in a few hours, but until then... the roaring feminist with an alibi was going to jail.

* * *

"Feminism...it's a state of mind.
The way we live now."— Anna Quindlen

The next morning, when Tracy arrived at the Montgomery apartment, his forensic team was hard at work combing the apartment for evidence. The apartment was large. It had at one time been two separate units, but someone had combined them, making one big unit that stretched almost the length of the building. The forensic team had split up into two groups, each taking one side. Tracy slipped on a pair of latex gloves and concentrated his search in the living room, in and around the chair where Randolph Montgomery had been found. Nothing had been moved. Everything was exactly as it had been when the police arrived.

Tracy decided now was the time to get a bit more aggressive. He moved the television opposite the chair, looked behind it, and then moved it back. The side table sitting beside the chair was next. He went through the drawers, but there was nothing interesting or significant—some old papers, a pair of glasses, a couple of out-of-date *TV Guides*, and a number two pencil. Tracy yelled to his team in the back of the apartment but didn't get an answer. He almost went to see if they were having any luck when something caught his eye. Something shiny underneath the chair. He slid the ottoman aside without moving the chair itself and reached under to extract the shiny object.

It was a watch. A gold watch. The face of the dial had been smashed. The hour and minute hands were barely visible behind the jagged web of cracked glass. Tracy carefully scratched away each of the little shards and set them aside. Once they were removed, he knew what he was staring at... the watch that Randolph Montgomery was wearing when he was killed. And the time he was murdered... 9:17 p.m.

* * *

Tracy arrived back at the precinct. He went directly into the interrogation room where Rose Thorne sat waiting. She was wearing a jailhouse jumpsuit, which—not surprisingly—looked good on her. When he opened the door, she was sitting with folded hands, just as before. The color in her face was a bit more pale and her eyes not quite so bright, but other than that... "I have some good news for you, Miss Thorne. You are getting out of here. Someone has sprung you."

The lovely face looked up into his. "My attorney finally came through?"

"No, ma'am. It wasn't your attorney."

"Then who?"

"Me."

Rose Thorne smiled.

"I guess I should thank you, Detective Tracy. What strings did you pull? Or did you have success in verifying my whereabouts? Success... nothing more than merely hanging on when others have let go. Or maybe you just came to your senses and realized I didn't do it after all?"

"I searched the apartment with my team of experts. No one had been in or out of that apartment since the night of the murder. I found Mr. Montgomery's watch. It shattered when he went to defend himself. It told the whole story. He was killed at 9:17. And I know for a fact you were at the lecture hall testing the camera at 9:07. You didn't have time to kill him and be back in time to make that tape. You are cleared, Miss Thorne. And I am sorry that you had to go through this. It's good news for you and bad news for me. Now I have to go out there and find the real killer."

"Maybe I can help, Detective."

"If you can... please do."

"I am not going to point fingers the way *my* accusers did. All I am going to say is... check into the business owned by the Beechers. Randolph's niece and her husband have a few problems and a lot of skeletons."

Tracy eyed Rose Thorne as he knocked on the door, signaling for the matron to escort her from the room. "As soon as I complete the paperwork, you will be out of here, Miss Thorne. I am sorry for any inconvenience. You are free to return to the apartment if you wish. My men are done."

"Thank you, Detective."

"And I have just one favor to ask, Miss Thorne... I feel I can ask since I'm the one who cleared you."

"Okay, what is it?"

"May I bring my cousin to meet you? She has been
to a few of the rallies, and she admires you very much. It
would be a thrill for her. We won't take up much of your
time."

Rose Thorne tried to conceal her obvious pleasure.
She held up one hand. "Say no more, Detective. Bring her
by the apartment the day after tomorrow. Around noon.
And now do *me* a favor... and please keep me informed as
to your progress in the case. I want you to catch Randolph's
killer and bring them to justice. Just remember what I said
about the Beechers..." And with that, Rose Thorne left the
room, with the matron trailing timidly behind. Exactly who
was escorting who here?

* * *

"The Future is Female"
— Madame Gandhi

At Rose Thorne's suggestion, Tracy decided to do a
little investigating into the Beechers' finances. After some
business research, Tracy found that the Beechers had
recently dissolved a partnership with a man named Gary
Loomis. The business had lasted almost thirteen years—an
ice age in terms of partnerships, which tended to melt after
three or four trips around the calendar. Tracy discovered
Mr. Gary Loomis had opened a new business... a women's
shoe store. He had a place over on First. So Tracy headed
in that direction.

* * *

After wading through a minefield of female feet and
cardboard shoe boxes, Tracy found Gary Loomis in a back
room doing the books for the store and wearing a look on
his face that said *this better be important.* He got the
message after Tracy showed the store owner his badge.

"Mr. Loomis, I'm Detective Tracy with N.Y.P.D. I wonder if I might have a word with you in regard to your former partners... the Beechers, Linda and Harry."

Loomis led the way into a quiet corner of the office and offered Tracy a seat. "What do you want to know, Detective? The partnership fizzled after thirty years."

"I understood it was thirteen years."

"It was. It just seemed like thirty... there's no love lost between me and the Beechers. But I've moved on with my life. I have the shoe store now."

"Do you know anything about their current situation? Are they in any kind of financial bind?"

"Yes. They are. They had to pay me off to get me out of the partnership. I've heard through the 'ladies-handbag-grapevine' that they aren't going to make it. I always told them we needed to modernize that old, outdated equipment. But they wouldn't listen. They would rather buy me out by mortgaging the house than by using their heads. But hey, I can't complain. I got my money back, and I'm out of the handbag business for good. Give me ladies' shoes and all those sweet little feet over purses any day."

* * *

Tracy left the shoe store, deep in thought. Okay... so the Beechers were in trouble. Interesting. They must have known Tracy would find out sometime. But was that a reason to kill Randolph Montgomery? They were the last ones to see him alive. Who would be stupid enough to make that statement if they were guilty? It's like a red flag that says: *hey, look at me... I'm over here.*

Tracy arrived back at the precinct. He went in through the front of the building but tiptoed past Chief Patton's door, hoping to go unnoticed. But it didn't work.

"Tracy, get in here. I want to see where you are
with the Montgomery case. Go get your notebook and bring
it in with you."

Tracy didn't feel up to a rehash of the case, but now
he had no choice. He would get through it. What did his
Uncle Petey always tell him... if you're going to play dumb,
you better get tough. Did he have something concrete? Say
yes and get grilled. Say no and the outcome is no different.
He grabbed his notes off his desk and headed back to the
chief's office. He must have looked like doom and gloom
when he lowered his frame down into the chair the precinct
boys had dubbed *the hot seat*. "Okay, Chief, what do you
want to know?"

"Who is your number one suspect currently? You
let the Thorne woman walk out the door, so you must have
someone else in mind. And this had better be good. But
don't be too hasty. Remember to let your thoughts soak in
your brain before they come out of your mouth."

"I'm thinking the niece and nephew—Linda and
Harry Beecher. They're having financial troubles, about to
lose their house, business is at a standstill... all of those
reasons add up quickly. We know now that Montgomery
was killed at 9:15. The Beechers said they left at 8:40, but
maybe they didn't. Maybe they stayed. Mabel Radcliff
didn't hear or see them leave. They knew Rose Thorne
wouldn't be back until after her lecture, so maybe they
waited until she was gone and then killed him."

"It's possible. Is there anyone else?"

"No. Both neighbors—the one next door and the
one across the hall—are above suspicion."

Chief Patton looked at Tracy with narrow eyes.
"That's all well and good, Detective. But I don't need to
tell you that sometimes the ones who are above suspicion
are the ones you have to watch. So go back and use those
famous instincts of yours. And most important of all... go
over the timeline and all the statements one more time.

Somewhere there's something too big to ignore..." Tracy nodded. Nothing more. "...Yeah, I know what you're thinking, Tracy. Easy for me to say. And you know that I can't explain what I just said any clearer. And even if I could, I don't think I want to. Just figure it out yourself. Remember—I'm not always right, but I'm never wrong..."

Sometimes a detective's greatest accomplishment is the ability to keep his mouth shut.

* * *

"Women hold up half the sky."
—Mao Zedong

TRACY'S TIMELINE: MONTGOMERY CASE

- **6:30 p.m.** — Beechers arrive at the Montgomery apartment for dinner.
- **8:20 p.m.** — Rose Thorne leaves for the rally, leaving the Beechers with Randolph Montgomery.
- **8:45 p.m.** — Beechers *claim* they left the apartment and went home. *(Did they?)*
- **9:07 p.m.** — Rose Thorne is seen testing the camera in the lecture hall.
- **9:17 p.m.** — Randolph Montgomery is killed. *(Time frozen by his shattered gold watch.)*
- **9:20 p.m.** — Rose Thorne begins her speech.
- **9:48 p.m.** — Rose Thorne ends her speech and leaves the stage.
- **10:10 p.m.** — Mabel Radcliff sees and hears Rose Thorne arrive home in a cab.
- **10:13 p.m.** — Mabel Radcliff sees Rose Thorne standing over the body.
- **10:16 p.m.** — Rose Thorne reports the murder to the police.

* * *

It all looked so simple. The coroner's report confirmed that Montgomery had been murdered sometime between 8:30 and 10:10 p.m. But the gold watch told a more precise truth: *9:17*. That smashed timepiece had become the definitive witness—its jagged hands frozen in the moment of death. And it fit perfectly into the timeline. So who could have entered the apartment between the time the Beechers claimed they left and Rose Thorne returned? If Randolph Montgomery had opened the door, it would have been for someone he knew. After all, he was found still sitting in the same chair where the Beechers said they'd left him—the easy chair in front of the television. That suggested he wasn't surprised. No sign of struggle. No signs of flight. If he had let the killer in, he had felt safe enough to sit back down and resume watching TV. That meant one thing: *he knew the killer.*

Since the watch was found under the chair, Tracy was convinced that Montgomery had been killed *right there*. He hadn't been attacked elsewhere and moved. There was *no blood splatter* in any other room. And the shattered watch suggested the first blow didn't kill him. He must have raised his arm to defend himself from the second strike, the moment that cracked the glass and locked the time into place. So, where did the guilty finger point? Who? Montgomery's niece and her husband? One of his female neighbors? Or someone else—someone who hadn't yet surfaced? *That unknown someone... that no one knows.*

* * *

"I'm a feminist. What's your superpower?"
—Anonymous

Tracy decided to go back, one more time, to see Mabel Radcliff. When he did, she informed him that the only people—other than the niece—who had been in and out of the Montgomery apartment since Rose Thorne moved in were people familiar with Randolph Montgomery. Tracy also questioned the time Rose Thorne came home.

"I saw her get out of the taxi, Detective. It was like around 10:10. She was singing to herself, I could hear her loud and clear through the open window and being in the front apartment and all. It was that Helen Reddy song, you know, the one... *I am woman, hear me roar...* or some such nonsense."

Mabel Radcliff was shaking her head when Tracy asked, "What about Deborah Ross, the neighbor across the way?"

Mabel pooh-poohed the idea of Deborah being a killer. "If Deb Ross was going to kill someone, she would put rat poison in a meatloaf—not bludgeon them over the head. And besides, Detective Tracy, she adored Randolph. And she liked Rose... why, I'm not sure."

"So what I think you're saying, Mrs. Radcliff, is that if Deborah Ross had killed anyone in that house, it would have been Rose Thorne. That would give her sole access to Mr. Montgomery." A thought was winding its way through Tracy's brain. Not a pretty thought. Was Deborah Ross trying to frame Rose Thorne for the murder she herself committed? Get her out of the way? But why? It wouldn't increase her inheritance from Randolph Montgomery. Or would it?

But Tracy didn't want to think badly of Deborah Ross. He wasn't sure why... maybe it was because she reminded him of his high school sweetheart. The one he let get away. Adrian Westhoff. She had wanted to get married right out of high school. He didn't. One night Adrian came to him—he remembered vividly how she turned to him and said:

"We could have had it all, Nick. All of it. Including the white picket fence. You a cop, me a fashion designer. I hope you find what you're looking for, because obviously I'm not it." And then she had walked out of his life forever.

He heard at the ten-year reunion that she ended up marrying Jimmie Long. He hated Jimmie Long. Today, he had to remember that a likeness to someone he had once cared for was no reason to clear someone of cold-blooded murder. And like it or not, that was exactly what he was doing.

* * *

"Feminists aren't anti-men…
They're pro-human."
—Anonymous

The next day, after a brief phone call and an open invitation, Tracy and his cousin Natalie showed up at the apartment of Rose Thorne and the late Randolph Montgomery. Natalie Delassandro was a cousin on his mother's side of the family. He had another cousin named Natalie, but this one was the favorite. She had married a great guy by the name of Joey Delassandro. Tracy and Nat, as he called her, had been more than cousins since childhood.

Rose Thorne was gracious, welcomed them with open arms, and directed them into the living room. The easy chair where Randolph Montgomery had died had been removed. In its place was a cushy loveseat with chintz pillows and a cozy leopard throw.

Natalie seemed in awe of the feminist spokeswoman. She told Rose that she had attended a few conferences where Rose was the speaker and that she was impressed enough to join the movement. Rose Thorne talked—lectured, almost. Her attitude seemed to say *notice how important I am*. And the two women completely ignored Tracy, who wandered around the apartment looking for something to read. He almost felt like he was looking for clues, which he wasn't, of course. He found a few magazines, some old photo albums—that sort of thing. Nothing of real interest.

Sometime later, Deborah Ross stopped by from across the hall and joined the discussion. Then, without warning, Tracy noticed something. He would say later that he recognized the shift in the atmosphere of the room. Natalie became increasingly quiet—not like herself at all. When Tracy finally gave the exit signal they had agreed upon, Nat seemed ready and willing. They both thanked Rose Thorne for her hospitality, said goodbye to Deborah Ross, and left the apartment hand in hand. When they got to the street, Tracy turned to Natalie with a questioning look. And what he saw in his cousin's eyes was something altogether unexpected. The next words out of her mouth were surprising—especially when you considered which of the two women she had just met was bothering her.

* * *

Nick Tracy woke up in the middle of the night. His bedside clock said 3:12 a.m. He was sweating. He threw off the covers and went to the kitchen for a glass of milk. Milk always seemed to calm him. A few of his four-legged friends padded after him, seemingly disgusted that they had been awakened in the middle of the night and needed to investigate where their master was going at such an ungodly hour. Winston, the mutt with a heart, seemed particularly put out by this intrusion. Even Bud and Lou spent a few minutes ruffling and unruffling their feathers in annoyance. Tracy ignored the animal protests and drank his milk in silence.

Something his cousin had said was on his mind. Something about the two women in the apartment earlier that night. Rose Thorne and Deborah Ross. Tracy felt as if he had heard one of the names before. Somewhere in his past—and nothing to do with this case. Neither woman was a suspect. They had both been cleared. But it was still there, in the back of his mind, gnawing at his conscience. Tracy finished the glass of milk in one long drink.

"Okay, guys. Let's go back to bed." The group once again followed in Tracy's footsteps as they all returned to their beds and snuggled in. Bogart let out one long *it's-about-time* groan as he wiggled around looking for that certain spot in his warm beanbag, unaware that his master was doing his best to clear his mind—even though he was sure there was something he was missing. *Something important.*

* * *

6:00 a.m. came too early. Tracy swung his legs over the side of the bed and rubbed the stubble on his face, like an old man emerging from a warm bath that had gone cold. A quick shower, a piece of toast with coffee, a snuggle with each of his buddies, and then he found himself driving to the precinct, *My Sharona* by The Knack blasting on the radio. What a way to start the day.

At Headquarters, Tracy tossed his coat onto his desk and headed to the file room. He wasn't sure exactly what he was looking for, but he knew if there was a link to the past, it could be found there in the moldy old files. When his search turned up nothing but more files, he headed to the office of the eldest detective in the Manhattan precinct—Joe Weber.

On the way to Weber's office, he passed Red Turner, an undercover cop who was going on a stakeout. He was dressed as a west side damsel in distress. Tracy couldn't resist. "Hey Red. The Avon lady called. She

123

doesn't want you to tell anyone where you buy your makeup."

There were some snickers among the rest of the precinct. Red showed Tracy one of his fingers and moved on, wobbling on high heels and pulling at the undergarments holding him and his bright yellow dress together. When Tracy turned and waltzed into Joe Weber's office, Joe was just putting his feet up on his desk, staring out the window at the city below.

"You know, Tracy... one of these days Red is going to pop you in the chops for teasing him. You may be covering his detail one day, and I have to say—Red looks a whole lot better in a dress than you do. Now, you want somethin', I can tell. What is it?"

"Just a trip into that memory bank of yours. The one where all the cases are stored. And don't send me to the file room. I've already been there. I'm wearing half the dust in that vault. I just want your first reaction to a couple of names. They aren't related. They aren't even connected."

"Okay, quit stalling and give them to me. I've got work to do."

"Deborah Ross. Rose Thorne."

Detective Joe Weber pulled his feet off the desk and pushed his chair back against the wall. The look on his face said it all. One of those names had hit a nerve. "Boy, you aren't kidding when you say they're not related. Two different cases."

"Cases? Which cases?"

"Nothing you might remember, Tracy. Happened years back. While you were working on the Brockmore case. There was a Deborah Ross who was part of a ring of forgers and con artists. They were working a few big marks back in the late sixties. Big ring. Lots of members. Mostly women. We broke up the group, sent a few of them to jail. But there were others, like the Deborah Ross I'm thinking of, who squirmed through the cracks. No evidence. Nothing to pin on her. So she got off scot-free. What has she done, by the way? More scams?"

"No. If it's her, she's just the neighbor of a murder victim. No evidence. No suspicion. Just a hunch about her relationship to the victim. And now... what about the name Rose Thorne?"

"Oh, Rose Thorne is a different story altogether. The Rose Thorne I'm thinking of was the girlfriend of a kingpin mobster who turned up dead in the East River. Big hit. She didn't have anything to do with the murder—we checked her out from both sides of Sunday. She had an airtight alibi. She'd never even met the guys who pulled off the murder. But she did testify at the trial. Beautiful girl. Nobody could forget the way she looked on that witness stand." Joe Weber pointed to one of the twenty framed newspaper clippings hanging on his wall above his desk. Detective Weber liked to keep clippings from his most famous collars. There was the face of a convicted killer, his eyes staring straight ahead in shock as he was being handcuffed and hauled away to prison. A convicted killer that Rose Thorne helped put away. "One of my better pieces of work, my friend."

Tracy thanked Weber and then left the man's office. As he walked back to his own office, Tracy had a few thoughts. His hunch hadn't panned out the way he had hoped. He was right back where he started from with:

    1.) A dead man
    2.) A murder weapon with no prints
    3.) A couple of innocent bystanders
    4.) No idea where to turn next

He was really leaning toward the Beechers being the most likely suspects. They had motive—money for their failing business. They had opportunity—last ones to see Montgomery alive. And they had no alibi other than a car trip home and an evening spent alone.

Tracy had just about decided to bring the Beechers into the precinct for questioning when the phone on his desk rang. Doris had put through an overly hysterical woman who needed Tracy *right now*. It was Mabel Radcliff.

"Okay, calm down, Mrs. Radcliff, and tell me again. What is it you remembered?"

"I can't believe that I didn't realize this from the very beginning. Why didn't I? It's crazy. I knew something was wrong. I didn't know what... but I knew it."

"And that something is?" Tracy prompted.

"It's the television, Detective. The television in Randolph's apartment. Now listen very carefully..."

By the time Tracy hung up the phone, he had a whole new idea that fit with everything he already knew. Put it all together, and you had one extremely clever killer.

* * *

"Rise of the woman. Rise of the nation."
—Madeleine Albright

Nick Tracy and his cousin Natalie Delassandro stood in the wings of the stage watching as Rose Thorne delivered her speech on feminist causes. She was an eloquent speaker. Her audience were her captives. It was more than thirty minutes before Thorne waved to the assembled masses—who were on their feet cheering—and then left the stage through the right-side portal. When she saw Tracy and his cousin waiting there, her eyes lit up in surprise.

"Hello, Detective. Ms. Delassandro... what a nice surprise."

Tracy's face was void of expression. His voice matched his face. "That was a very inspirational speech you delivered tonight, Miss Thorne. You deserved that standing ovation. But your next gig may not be possible."

Rose Thorne laughed out loud. "Don't be silly, Detective. *Not possible*, meaning impossible? Really? The word literally says *I'm possible*. Didn't you listen to my speech?"

Rose Thorne suddenly had an expression of skepticism regarding this unannounced visit and the heaviness of the air. She looked around and turned to Tracy with a questioning look. "I never knew, Detective. Since when did you become interested in feminist causes?"

Tracy didn't hesitate, and his eyes never left those of the feminist. "Since you killed Randolph Montgomery, Miss Thorne."

* * *

Nick Tracy and Natalie were lunching in the back of the Chelsea Café—a favorite of his.

"Okay, Nick. You promised to tell me how she did it, if I promised not to ask you until we got here. So, here we are."

"It was simple. Rose Thorne and Randolph Montgomery had dinner with the Beechers. Then, at 8:20 or so, Rose leaves the apartment for the rally and her speaking engagement. But instead of leaving, she walks out the door and waits at the end of the hallway, hidden in the recess that runs past Deborah Ross's apartment. She was banking on the Beechers leaving shortly after she did. And she was right. They left the apartment around 8:40. And that's when Rose went back into the apartment and killed Randolph Montgomery. She left the murder weapon there just in case someone found him before she got back. And then she turned his watch ahead half an hour and smashed it—probably with her foot—and hid it under the chair for the police to find. Then she went to the lecture hall and gave her speech, knowing that Eric Rawlings would be filming her and that the video would show the times she was on stage. The test run put her there at almost the exact time that showed on the smashed watch. When the lecture was over, she took a cab back to the apartment, making sure that Mabel Radcliff heard her get out of the cab singing. Of course, she picked the Helen Reddy song so Mabel wouldn't have any doubt it was her. The added bonus was having Mabel show up on the doorstep so quickly. It proved there wasn't enough time for her to have killed her husband. I think she loved it when everyone said she must have done it—Mabel Radcliff, Deborah Ross, the Beechers, even Montgomery's attorney—because she knew that when one of the cops found the smashed watch, she would be cleared."

"So what gave you the idea that she did it? Was it my comment that night when we left her apartment? When I said I didn't like her? That maybe the whole feminist thing was a front?"

"Maybe. Or it might have been that same night while you ladies were talking. I thumbed through a few of Rose Thorne's photo albums on her coffee table. I saw a picture of a man that looked familiar to me. The reason the man looked familiar is because I have seen that picture on the wall in Detective Weber's office a hundred times, without realizing what I was seeing. Rose was involved in the case. An eyewitness. She testified, but she lied. She said she didn't know the killer. But her album had several pages of photos with her and the killer at the same table— sometimes in an embrace." Tracy smiled, like he had a hidden secret he was about to reveal. "But the final blow was delivered by Mabel Radcliff. It had to do with the television set in Randolph Montgomery's apartment—the one that was so loud that Mabel and her husband always knew what Randolph Montgomery watched each night."

"What do you mean?"

"When Mabel walked in and found Rose standing over the body, the television was turned to CBS and *Dallas*.

I corroborated that statement myself. I'm the one who turned off the set when I arrived. *Dallas* was in the final scene. Mabel told me in no uncertain terms that Randolph Montgomery was a real stickler with his shows. On Friday nights, he watched *The Incredible Hulk* at 8:00 on CBS but always turned it to another show at 9:00 because *The Dukes of Hazzard* was next in the lineup, and then *Dallas* at 10:00—and he hated both of those shows. According to Mabel, he thought *Dukes* was cornball hillbilly stuff and always considered *Dallas* a stupid, over-dramatic soap opera."

"So what Randolph Montgomery was watching was more of an indicator of what time he was killed than the smashed watch?"

"I'm sure Rose Thorne forgot this one thing when she left the house after killing him. His favorite show, *The Incredible Hulk*, was playing nice and loud, but it only had another five or ten minutes to run. If Randolph had been alive at 9:00, he would have switched the channels. He never would have sat through *Dukes* and *Dallas*."

"Very good detective work, cousin. I'm impressed."

"Good. I want you to be impressed. But I have to admit one thing. Everyone else in this case was right and I was wrong. They were all certain she did it. I couldn't find a way... until I could. But you were a big help."

"Of course I was. We were a team, like Astaire and Rogers. The only thing is... even though old Fred gets all the accolades, Ginger did all those steps just like Freddie. And she did them backwards—and in heels."

* * *

EPILOGUE

Tracy and his cousin left the small café arm in arm. Natalie turned left; her husband John was waiting at the curbside not five yards away. He waved, Nick waved. And

then Tracy turned right, headed to his car parked in the
opposite direction parallel to the bodega storefront. He
threw the doggie bag into the back seat and made the drive
to his apartment in record time.

Once upstairs, he opened the door and walked in
just in time to have a talk with Butch Adams, the young
man who had been hired to care for his menagerie of
animals while Tracy was at work. And quite a menagerie it
was.

Currently, in addition to his first love, *Bogart* the
English bulldog, there were two Pomeranians he had
acquired when a neighbor skipped town. He named
them *George and Gracie*. A small mutt he had found
roaming the streets he called *Winston*. A pair of cockatoos
that had been left on his doorstep (he felt as if they were
both male and had named them *Bud and Lou*). A small
wire-haired terrier who somehow answered to the name
Greta Garbo. A couple of rare lizards with black beards in
a glass terrarium that became *Fred and Ethel*. And a tabby
cat that had a mind of his own that Tracy had tagged *Peter
Lorre*. (Tracy had discovered that unlike dogs who came
when you called, cats took a number and got back to you
later.) All in all, quite a motley crew with an owner who
could not resist taking in every poor creature who needed
love and a place to sleep. Tracy always tried to find homes
for the strays, but most of the time—like now—he ended
up keeping the neediest. A revolving door of creatures big
and small.

When Butch finally left for home, Tracy dialed a
number from his black book, another cousin in a sea of
cousins. Like the menagerie of animals, the cousins always
needed something, and most came to him when the need
was the greatest: a place to crash, a shoulder to cry on, a bit
of legal advice (as if he was a lawyer disguised as a cop,
like *Perry Mason* in reverse). And when there was a
possible murder. *Like now.*

EDGAR ALLAN POE WOULD BE PROUD

PROLOGUE

"The past is a pebble in my shoe."
—E.A. Poe

Most of the following happened just as it is written. Some happened more, some happened less. And there are those who would dispute the whole thing altogether. But when it came down to it, no one could dispute the fact that the service for Reverend Edward Lovett Smith was well attended by all who knew him or knew of him: the ministers in the surrounding areas, his parishioners, the babies he had baptized, the couples he had joined in holy matrimony, the members of his church staff, and of course, his wife Catherine, who was alone in the world now, as Edward Lovett Smith had been unable to produce an heir. But Catherine had been at peace with this fact, and lovingly doted on her minister husband, giving him the attention she would have heaped upon all those children she was never going to have. But Catherine Smith was holding a secret.

Catherine knew something about the man lying peacefully in that coffin made of the finest mahogany—

something she doubted anyone else in the room knew. It was a dark secret. A secret borne of the one flaw that Edward Lovett Smith had possessed: the man had been a victim of intense, raging, and uncontrollable jealousy.

Catherine Smith was not a raving beauty. She was very nice looking; perhaps one would say she resembled Harriet Nelson, or June Cleaver, or maybe Donna Reed—one of those TV show mothers, prim, proper, dressed modestly in the semi-frumpy style of the day. But it didn't matter to Edward Lovett Smith. He saw her as Marilyn Monroe standing over that grate in Times Square, her dress blowing up around her waist, showing all the world her long limbs shimmering in the light of the flashbulbs going off around her.

Yes, the Methodist preacher with the myopic eyesight saw his wife as a goddess. Nothing less. Even though most of the people in Edward Smith's life knew nothing about his raging jealousy, they had known two things about the good preacher. Number one: he was a scholar of Edgar Allan Poe; had read everything Poe had ever written and had done extensive research into the man's life and times. He quoted Poe in his sermons, in his everyday life, even in his rambling sleep talking. Yes, Edward Smith had been a Poe-aphile, and if there had been such a thing as a degree in *Poe-ism*, he would have possessed it. Number two: Edward Lovett Smith had an extremely weak heart, which the doctors told his mother when he was born would not hold out until his thirtieth birthday. But little Eddie had proven them all wrong. That defective heart held up until age forty-two, when it simply stopped. Just like the doctors had predicted. Yes, it just stopped.

And now Reverend Smith lay in a coffin, unmoving, deader than a doornail, as Poe would have said. What a pity. What a shame. Even though most people would agree he had led a good life—even though Edward

Lovett Smith himself was the least interesting part of his life.

And in a different story, in a different lifetime, maybe the Lord would have seen fit to give Edward Smith a healthy ticker, and he would be up right now giving Satan a run for his money at Sunday service. Fire and brimstone, and the eternal damnation of all those who went against the word of the Lord. Instead... well, it was a real shame. And now, if only that same good Lord had told the Reverend Edward Lovett Smith that his day of reckoning was coming soon, and that he would be lying in that beautiful mahogany coffin surrounded by all those people—perhaps then he might never have killed Tom Langley.

* * *

"I do not suffer from insanity.
I enjoy every minute of it."
—E.A. Poe

WEEKS EARLIER

The events as Reverend Edward Lovett Smith saw them

The good Reverend Edward Smith had fallen into mediocrity, having no alternative. Today, he had finished delivering his sermon on the evils of drink: one of his favorite subjects. However, he was starting to think that perhaps it was time to broaden his thinking about this particular sin; just not today. *Oh no, not today.*

Edward Smith was a tall, thin man of medium build, with dark eyes that sometimes appeared lit from within— like the good Lord's word was seeping through his soul and exiting his pupils. Smith was nice looking in the way that Jimmy Stewart in his younger years was nice looking. He wasn't considered debonair, nothing close to handsome.

But the more you were around him, the more he grew on you. If he had been a jingle, you would have a hard time getting his tune out of your head. He grew up an only child who graduated high school at an early age and then lost both of his parents when he was in seminary school; a terrible car crash on the BQE that sent their vehicle into a tailspin, colliding with an oncoming truck. Edward had been devastated and had taken to spending all his spare time with his aunt and uncle in Brooklyn: Christmas, Thanksgiving, Easter, birthdays. His father's brother and his wife were always there for him, with a small bedroom made up and waiting whenever the notion struck. The pair doted on him and tried to make up for his loss, but no one could do that.

And then Edward met Catherine Mary McDonald at the corner of 59th Avenue and Lexington. He had been wandering around Bloomingdale's, searching for a gift for his Aunt Helen, and there she was—a lovely young woman in a purple dress, just waiting for a customer to come by and relieve her of her boredom. At first, the sweet young lady with the green eyes and Irish face wanted little to do with the brash and lanky Edward Smith, who seemed to be obsessed with Edgar Allan Poe. Catherine rebuffed his advances, wouldn't take his phone calls. She insisted to him, and no doubt to herself, that she was only a counter girl at Bloomie's until the job she was waiting for in advertising came along. She told Edward that she had graduated from NYU with a nice little degree and spent every free moment applying for jobs at some of the major advertising firms in the city.

And then one day, while she was dodging Edward Smith's advances, Catherine got the call. It wasn't what she wanted—she was a bit disappointed—but she took the job as a clerk at an ad agency just to get her size-six shoe in the revolving door. She had dinner with Smith and told him she planned on moving up the corporate ladder. That, unfortunately, wasn't going to happen.

And while Catherine Mary McDonald learned a lesson, day by day, about capitalism in America, Edward Lovett Smith spent his free time breaking down the little clerk's defenses, like Jericho taking down that stubborn wall. One day, Catherine Mary McDonald woke up and realized that Edward Smith, the newly ordained minister of All Saints Church, was more of a source of income than the Sampson and Ashley Ad Agency, where she would be nothing more than a clerk for the rest of her days there. They were married soon after in a lovely church service.

And now, on this fine morning, Edward Smith was shaking hands with his loyal parishioners as they filed out of the double church doors. It was the least he could do, as they had sat quietly through most of his well-rehearsed sermon—except for the Lawrence boy, who fidgeted and sniffled almost constantly. (But Reverend Smith was passionate and forgiving of his parishioners. Even little Bobby Lawrence.) "Good to see you, Miss Olson. How is the bursitis? … Hello, Mr. Wallace. Glad to see you up and at 'em. … Oh, Miss Retz, is your husband feeling better? I see he's not here today..."

And then Edward Lovett Smith saw something out of the corner of his eye, over in the church garden. His wife was talking to Thomas Langley; their heads close together, their eyes all misty, like smoke from a distant fire. And they seemed to be whispering like there was no one else in the world. A little too chummy for the pastor's taste. Since Thomas Langley was his good friend, Reverend Smith knew Langley was a ladies' man—handsome, charming, and recently single after breaking up last week with his girlfriend of six years. Smith also knew that Langley considered married women easy prey, as they were almost always in need of attention.

Edward Lovett Smith left the church steps after his last parishioner departed, the last hand shaken. He observed Langley leaving in his car and Catherine heading back into the church to clean up the pews, pick up the hymnals. When he re-entered the church, Reverend Smith confronted his wife. He told Catherine he did not trust Langley. Catherine said that was crazy, as she and Langley were talking about her mother. And even if he did try something, she would not be interested. Smith said he didn't know if she was strong enough to resist Langley, or that Langley was strong enough to resist her. He told her that he was going to invite Langley to meet him at the church the following night and have a talk with him, and that he was bringing along some Scotch: Thomas Langley's weakness.

Catherine tried to talk her husband out of this idea. It was a bad one. And before they left the empty church, she reminded him to cover the baptismal tank; she had just put some chlorine in the tank to keep it clean. But the last thing on the good preacher's mind was the baptismal tank and the amount of chlorine it did or did not have. He was wondering how Poe would have written the conclusion of this situation. Where did he get his ideas for *The Pit and the Pendulum*, or *The Tell-Tale Heart*? Which gave Edward Lovett Smith an idea of his own.

* * *

*"Years of love have been forgotten
in the hatred of a minute."—E.A. Poe*

The events as Thomas Langley, the victim, saw them

Thomas Langley had always had his eye on Catherine Smith. Yes, she was the wife of one of his good friends, but as they say: all is fair in love and war. However, this, of course, was neither. Thomas Langley didn't love Catherine and was certainly not prepared to go to war over her. He was just a little more than fond of her. She was attractive and smart and way too good for the likes of his pastor friend. But Thomas Langley knew better than to try and approach Catherine in a familiar sort of way. That would have been friendship suicide. Edward Smith would never have forgiven him any indiscretion. And Thomas Langley knew about Smith's jealous streak.

Langley had been an ear for the man on more than one occasion, where Smith would vent his imagined sightings of his wife being unfaithful—not physically, but in her mind. Langley knew his friend was unreasonably jealous and possessive. Smith's imagination would run wild: there was something going on behind his back, Catherine desired some man, the man was younger or better looking or wealthier. The list went on and on. So no, Thomas Langley knew better than to approach his friend's wife. He knew not to smile at her, not to compliment her or give her a hand up the church steps. Not to brush by her in the hallway or sit on her side of the table when he was invited for dinner.

But on this warm Sunday morning, Thomas Langley forgot himself. Maybe he was thinking that Edward was busy with church business and wouldn't notice. But for whatever reason, he made the supreme mistake of not only approaching Catherine but speaking with her in hushed tones about how he liked her new permed hair. Okay, so yes, he had quoted his hero, Edgar Allan Poe, who said that *the best things in life make you sweaty*—perhaps hoping to jolt her into the realization that they were actually talking together on the church grounds—but then he saw Edward watching them out of the corner of his eye. Not good. He ended the conversation abruptly and headed to his car. He knew Edward was going to be angry. He just hoped the man wouldn't take it out on his wife. But of course he knew he would.

So he wasn't too surprised when Catherine called him later that night while her husband was holding a meeting of church officials, to tell him that Edward saw them together and was angry and was going to ask him to meet at the church. A meeting? What for? Just to rant and rave and tell him not to go near Catherine again? Smith could do that on the telephone. So why a meeting in person?

Langley thanked Catherine for the warning and then hung up the phone. He would be ready for Smith, ready with an explanation. He was a smart man—he would think of something plausible. And if necessary, he would declare his innocence repeatedly. (This reminded Langley of what was considered the cleverest of all Poe stories: *The Cask of Amontillado*, where the main character had his friend help him build a wall and then sealed him inside.) Yes, Langley told himself, he would think of something to say to his long-time friend. A friend who knew him years before, back when.

Thomas Langley and Edward Smith met in a literary class based on the writings of Edgar Allan Poe, an American short story writer who shocked the society of his day with his outlandish and frightening tales of murder and horror in all sorts of unusual settings. *Macabre* was Poe's genre—the more grisly, the more unlikely, the better. Smith and Langley had shared the love of the man's writings, so much so that they had spent many a night over a glass of beer discussing the "Master of Mystery" a few blocks from the NYU campus. When Smith had finished his tenure at the seminary school and had joined All Saints Methodist Church in Manhattan, he had persuaded Langley to join the congregation. And Langley had caved. He hadn't been much of a churchgoer in his life, but it sounded like it might be a good idea. Just in case.

And then he used the church for his own personal dating service. There were a good many women who attended All Saints. Some were good looking. Thomas Langley had started taking his pick. And now he had been seen cozying up to his best friend's wife on the church lawn. Still as bad an idea as six hours ago. All that was left for him to do was to go to meet Smith and convince him that he had no designs on his wife—or any other woman for that matter. *Edgar Allan would have loved this little melodrama.*

Thomas Langley walked across the room to his television set and turned the channel to the local news and then situated himself on the overstuffed sofa. There would be time to come up with some sort of lie before he went to meet Smith. In the meantime, there was no use worrying about something that hadn't even happened. Maybe Catherine was just being dramatic. She could be like that sometimes. Maybe it was all just nonsense.

Langley nestled down into the soft cushions and closed his eyes. He remembered that Poe had once said, *"A wise man hears one word and understands two."* And this little situation would have been a good start to a Poe story. And Thomas Langley knew it. Of course, he couldn't imagine what was about to happen. Oh, no. Not by a mile. Because, as his hero E. A. Poe once said, *"The invisible things in life are the only realities."* And he was about to get a big dose of his own invisibility.

* * *

*"Believe only half of what you see and
nothing of what you hear."*
—E.A. Poe

The events as Catherine Smith, the witness, saw them

Catherine Smith was an attractive woman in her mid-forties, with dark brown hair and green eyes the color of shamrocks. Her smile was wide and strong; it could win an argument with little to go on. And she admired her husband—even though she was never going to have children.

Edward Lovett Smith was unable to procreate. It was a flaw that had been a constant topic of conversation up until two years ago, when Edward came home from a pastoral retreat in Montpellier and told Catherine that he never wanted to speak of the topic again. And he hadn't. He had never said the word 'children' or 'sterile' or any word associated with the two since that day. And Catherine knew better than to go against her husband's wishes. He was, after all, the spiritual leader of a congregation that, at one time, had even included a President of the United States. (In 1974, Gerald Ford had to remain in New York to address the General Assembly at the United Nations and had attended their humble church on Sunday morning. Mr. and Mrs. Ford had been cordial and a pure delight.)

So, Catherine Smith was quite settled and content with her life. She organized fundraisers, bake sales, the children's Christmas program, and all of the other duties expected of a pastor's wife. And she accomplished them all with a smile. But like all dutiful wives, there came a time when enough was not enough. Catherine Mary McDonald had given up a career in advertising—as meager as it was at the time—and had given herself wholeheartedly to the job of nurturing and supporting her fire-and-brimstone husband. It wasn't what she had hoped for; her degree from NYU was just a piece of paper inside a frame collecting dust now. But hey, who wouldn't want to be in her tiny little size 6 shoes? She would never have to want for anything. But maybe that was the point. Maybe she *wanted* to want. But then, of course, no one asked her what she wanted. So Catherine Mary McDonald Smith carried on with her day-to-day life. Until...

It was flattering that someone paid attention to her. And of course, it didn't hurt that Thomas Langley was handsome and charming. But on the other hand, it did hurt that he was her husband's best friend.

* * *

Catherine stood inside the now-empty church. It felt hollow. The sound of her high heels clicking on the wood floor echoed through the rafters. She stopped for a moment, thinking. Then started up again, collecting the hymnals and picking up the discarded prayer cards. She even found some bubble gum stuck to a wrapper and kicked under a pew. She knew who had discarded the gum, of course. Jimmy Burton had to be the culprit. She had observed his chewing during the service. His moving jaw stuck out like the distraction that it was. She picked up the wrapper and deposited it in the sack she was carrying.

Once the trash was cleared away and the hymnals returned to the holders on the back of each pew, Catherine started for the front of the church. And that was when she heard her husband of eighteen years as he entered through the back door. By the sound of his footsteps—quick and precise—he was angry or had something on his mind. His first words were crisp and short. "Catherine, why do you let yourself be seen with Thomas Langley? He is disgraceful. Not a man of God, even though he comes to service every week. I swear he only comes to scout out the women— who's wearing short skirts, makeup..."

Catherine was appalled. "Really, Edward. That is not a nice thing to say about one of your good friends who..."

"Stop right there, Cathy. You don't know what that man is capable of. I do. I want you to stay away from him. It's not proper for the minister's wife to be seen with another man. Alone."

Catherine Smith nodded, as she always did when her husband's bouts of jealousy were at the forefront of their conversation. "Okay, Ed. Even though there was nothing to be concerned about. We were only talking about my mother and my macramé class. I will refrain from speaking with Thomas. Will that make you happy?"

"Yes. It will. The only problem is... I don't know if the damage is already done. I don't think you are strong enough to resist his advances, his fake debonair charms. And I don't know if he is strong enough to resist *you*."

"Don't be absurd, Ed."

Edward Lovett Smith shook his head from side to side. "You know what Poe said about lying, Catherine: *A lie can travel around the world while truth is putting her shoes on.* So, don't think you can lie to me about anything to do with Thomas Langley... my good friend. In fact, I think I need to speak to Thomas alone, while the incident is fresh. I am going to ask him to meet me here in the church. I will bring along a bottle of Scotch. He can't resist a drink—one drink and he's soused. And then I'll know what he has in mind when it comes to my wife."

"Is this really necessary, Edward? I mean..."

"It's not only necessary, but also imperative. Please don't ask me again. And now, let's go home for a bite to eat. I think we still have some ham left. And we have time to feed the rose bushes."

Catherine nodded and followed in her husband's wake as they started down the aisle. She looked back once to make sure she had accomplished everything she had set out to do. *Oh, one more thing.* She turned to her husband as he held the door open to the front vestibule. "Speaking of— Ed, don't forget to cover the baptismal tank. I added chlorine a few minutes ago, but I think I forgot to put the top back on."

The pastor nodded, but Catherine had a feeling that he had heard little of what she had said, and none of what she had meant.

* * *

"The believer is happy; the doubter is wise."
—E.A. Poe

The events as Nick Tracy, the detective, saw them

Arianna Adams had been a member of the All Saints Methodist Church in Manhattan for more than twenty years. She even worked in the church's main office, helping with the accounting and church fundraisers. Arianna enjoyed her job, which was much more rewarding than sitting at home watching game shows and soap operas on the television. And she had become quite good at her duties. At least the pastor said so. And even though the pay was lousy and the hours miserable, she came to work with a smile and a bright, sunny attitude that sometimes annoyed everyone around her. So when Reverend Edward L. Smith died suddenly, Arianna was quite alarmed. Sure, she knew about the bad heart—everyone knew—but no one seemed the slightest bit concerned before, including the pastor himself or his wife, Catherine. And now he was gone.

One day after the funeral, with a bit of reluctance, Arianna called her cousin, who she remembered was a handsome police detective, and left a message for him to call her that night. When he did, she told him that she needed some help; she had a strong suspicion that there was evil at work regarding the death of Pastor Smith, and could he send someone over so she could explain. If anyone could help her and come up with an answer, Arianna knew it would be Detective Nick Tracy. And that was how the New York City homicide detective got involved in a case that was one of the most puzzling of his career.

* * *

Tracy looked over the death certificate and the autopsy report. There was nothing to indicate that Edward Lovett Smith had died of anything other than a heart attack. No hint of foul play. No suspicions by anyone, including the coroner and the police. The man had possessed a weak heart as a child. He had been under some stress lately. He had died at home. Tracy couldn't find anything in the official file to support cousin Arianna's "bad feeling" that something wasn't right and that the pastor had met his Maker before his appointed time. But where there was smoke, there was fire.

The church office was "open" for questions when Detective Tracy walked inside the rectory that bright spring morning. He interrogated everyone present. Each of them had an answer for where they were and what they were doing when Reverend Smith died. Everyone, that is, except for the assistant pastor, Harold Raymond. Harold Raymond, according to Arianna, disliked Pastor Smith. He wanted his job. Raymond's wife had run away. He was understandably angry at the world and everyone in it—including God—and apparently, to Harold Raymond's way of thinking, becoming head pastor of All Saints Church would fix everything wrong in his life. Tracy wondered if maybe the assistant pastor had put a substance in Reverend Smith's drink that acted on his heart. He decided to investigate and see for himself, starting with the medical examiner. But his efforts would prove fruitless. The toxicology report showed there was nothing out of the ordinary found in Reverend Smith's lifeless body.

Tracy called on the assistant pastor's home the next day and was shown into a small living room with bowling trophies lining one wall and pictures of Jesus lining the other. When Harold Raymond joined him, he was cordial enough, but not friendly. He answered Tracy's questions, his eyes staring straight into the detective's without wavering. Still, Tracy had to agree with Arianna's assessment that something felt "off" about the assistant pastor's demeanor.

Later that afternoon, Tracy stopped into the church office and spoke with everyone once more. That's when he learned the assistant pastor had been stealing money from the church account, which consisted of funds collected each Sunday in the offering plates. One of the secretaries broke down and spilled the beans. She knew that Raymond had helped himself to the funds on more than one occasion. She had even been a witness to the theft. She was sure there were more times but couldn't prove it.

Tracy brought Raymond into the station for questioning and fingerprinting. While he was in the interrogation room, one of the precinct's detectives went back to the Raymond home and snooped around in the structure Tracy had observed in the backyard. The detective found a container of arsenic in the corner of the old shed. When confronted, Raymond said it was to kill gophers, but there were no gopher holes in the yard. In the meantime, Tracy had one of the other detectives look into Raymond's past. The assistant pastor had a record: vehicular manslaughter. Raymond had been convicted but only served five years. While in prison, it was said that he "got religion."

Catherine Smith, the dead pastor's wife, told Tracy that Reverend Smith trusted Raymond and never suspected him of anything. But when Tracy asked Raymond where he was the night Reverend Smith had his heart attack, the assistant pastor could not come up with an answer. And when asked about the missing money, once again, no probable explanation. Tracy told Raymond that although he had no proof the man had anything to do with Reverend Smith's death, he would still have to appear before a judge on the theft charges if the church wanted to press charges.

And they did. The Ecumenical Council had a rule book of church policies. The discipline would be merciful but strict. After serving any sentence handed down, Assistant Pastor Raymond would be transferred to another church in a lesser capacity. He would never be allowed to handle church funds again. The Ecumenical Council's ruling was unwavering.

Tracy was disappointed that he couldn't find any solid evidence of the assistant pastor's guilt when it came to the passing of Pastor Smith. He had wanted to help his cousin, but there was nothing concrete enough to bring to the D.A.—nothing that would hold up in court. The man may have been guilty of theft, but there was no evidence of murder.

Tracy expressed his apologies to Arianna the day after Harold Raymond was charged and told her to contact him if any evidence came to light. He left his card on the church clerk's desk. "You never know, Arianna. Things have a way of showing up later. So if you hear anything, please let me know."

Of course, Tracy would never hear anything—because there was nothing to hear. Harold Raymond had nothing whatsoever to do with the stopping of Reverend Edward Lovett Smith's heart.

* * *

"False hope is nicer than no hope at all."
—E.A. Poe

The events as Judge Wendal Scardello saw them

The case of the missing church funds at the All Saints Church came before Wendal Scardello on a Monday morning. Harold Raymond was charged with stealing a large amount of money from the church funds. The amount was anywhere between $60,000 and $70,000. Harold Raymond pleaded innocent. However:

1.) Investigators found Raymond's fingerprints on items in the church safe.
2.) Several of the secretaries in the church office found discrepancies in the church's financial journals.
3.) Raymond made some large deposits into his personal bank account—in cash.
4.) Raymond was the only one handling the books at the time the money went missing.

Harold Raymond's attorney explained these deposits to the judge as personal loans from friends. The defense brought in the "friends," who testified that they did indeed loan Raymond money on occasion. With that, the defense had established a reasonable doubt. No one was called to testify who had actually seen Raymond steal the money. So there must have been that hint of doubt in Judge Wendal Scardello's mind as he acquitted Harold Raymond on the single count of theft. The judge then ordered Raymond to community service for the next twelve months in exchange for the acquittal.

"You got off easy, Mr. Raymond. This is not your first time before a court, but I didn't have any solid proof of your guilt. You will serve the sentence of community service for twelve months, and then I'm guessing you will be asked to make restitution to your church as they see fit. But just remember this: if there is a next time, you will not get off so easily, as this incident will be attached to your permanent record."

The assistant pastor walked out of the courtroom and gave Tracy, who was sitting in the back, the evil eye. But Tracy barely noticed. He was thinking that this was a case of his being unable to do his job. He couldn't find any evidence that Raymond had hastened the death of Rev.

Smith—but somehow, he knew there was something there.
But oh, how wrong he was. It was one of the few times
when the NYPD detective was so far off the track, he was
on another train. But Tracy would never know that. In fact,
no one ever would.

* * *

"I became insane, with long intervals
of horrible sanity."—E.A. Poe

The events as the Good Lord in Heaven saw them

That fateful night, Catherine Smith called Thomas
Langley the moment her husband, Edward Smith, left the
house with the bottle of Scotch. He was heading to the
church to wait for Langley, hoping to get him to talk about
his intentions toward Catherine. The pastor knew Langley
couldn't hold his liquor, and that one glass of the five-year-
old Scotch would loosen the man's lips. It all sounded so
ominous. But it really wasn't. However, the good pastor
didn't know that.

On the phone, Catherine told Langley that she had
emptied the bottle of Scotch while her husband was in the
shower and replaced the liquor with weak tea. After a brief
conversation, Langley thanked Catherine for the
information and hung up. He headed out the door to his car
and drove the short distance to All Saints Church.

Reverend Smith was waiting for him up by the altar.
The two men sat down in chairs situated just behind the
pulpit where Smith stood every Sunday preaching, with the
Almighty on his left shoulder whispering in his ear. It was
God's word he wanted to feel, and God's word he got.
Smith likened himself to the burning bush, where God
spoke directly to Moses so there would be no bad
communication.

However, today Reverend Smith was in another dimension. He wasn't taking orders from God. He just hoped God would forgive him for what he was about to do. Or was he going to Hell on a broomstick, as his uncle used to warn? Maybe, the way he figured it, he'd have enough time to explain everything to St. Peter when he got to Heaven.

Thomas Langley watched as Edward Smith poured a tall drink of the golden liquid from the Scotch bottle. Smith didn't take a drink himself, and Langley didn't expect him to. (Langley had learned back at NYU that Smith was allergic to alcohol. It made him violently ill.) But Langley wanted to know what Smith was up to, so he pretended to get tipsy from the weak tea, intentionally slurring his words and stumbling around the altar.

Thinking he had Langley right where he wanted him, Smith started to ask questions. "Do you have a thing for my wife, Langley?"

"Yeah, maybe I do. But I would never try anything…"

"I don't believe you. You're a scoundrel."

"What? Are you nuts, Smith? I said I wasn't going to do anything, although we both know I could. I mean, look at you and look at me. Who do you think women find attractive, huh?"

Edward Smith had heard enough. The righteous reverend lunged at Langley and grabbed him around the throat. He began to choke him while dragging him sideways at the same time. The baptismal tank, built into the raised platform of the pulpit, was only a few feet away. If Smith thought Langley was as drunk as he appeared, it would just be a matter of getting him into the tank and holding him underwater for a few minutes.

Langley fell backward into the tank easily. The splash caused the water to overflow onto the pulpit. *The water can be cleaned up later* was the only thought

Reverend Edward Smith had as he continued to choke the man, holding him under. Langley flailed, as if helpless to do anything more. The struggle was almost over when Smith heard it: the sound of the back door opening and footsteps approaching. He was sure he had locked that door, but—

"Edward! What are you doing? For God's sake, stop! You're going to kill him." It was only seconds before Catherine was by her husband's side. Smith let go of Thomas Langley and stared down at the limp body floating on the surface of the baptismal water. Catherine reached down and felt for Langley's pulse. She whirled around. "You've done it this time, Edward. He's dead." Smith backed away from the tank and his hysterical wife. "Run, Edward. Go get some blankets from the linen cupboard in the back of the Sunday School playroom. What you've done here is wrong, but what's done is done. We can't change that."

Blindly, Edward Smith did as he was told. When he returned with the blankets, Catherine had already pulled Langley from the water. She grabbed one from his hands and wrapped it around Thomas Langley's head and torso as quickly as she could. It was as if she couldn't bear to stare into those lifeless eyes.

She turned to her husband. "We'll put him in the back of your car and drive him to the YMCA behind the church. We'll throw him in the pool. If I know you, you gave him enough Scotch to kill a horse. It'll look like he came to visit you, got drunk again, stumbled behind the church, and drowned. Remember, I just filled this tank with chlorine. So the coroner won't know the difference. There'll be chlorinated water in his lungs. It'll appear he drowned in pool water."

"But what about—"

"His family? You know he doesn't have anyone. And what friends, other than you? When the YMCA staff finds him and calls the police, it'll just be a case of a terrible accident."

Edward Smith stared at his wife. The plan was brilliant. Where did she get these street smarts all of a sudden? Ellery Queen? Raymond Chandler? Edgar Allan Poe?

The two carried the lifeless body of Thomas Langley out the back door and into the trunk of Edward Smith's car. They drove around to the YMCA. It wasn't easy, but they managed to get Langley's body into the connecting yard and into the pool, carefully unwrapping the blankets and rolling him into the water. They hurried away quickly and tossed the wet blankets into the backseat. They'd deal with them later.

On the way home, not a word passed between husband and wife. It was almost as if they were thinking entirely different thoughts. And they were—*unbelievably* different.

* * *

EPILOGUE

"...Sayeth the raven: 'Nevermore.'"
—E.A. Poe

The events as the Devil himself saw them

Over the next few days, Edward Lovett Smith's life became one miserable event after another. He couldn't sleep. He couldn't eat. He barely left the house except on Sundays. He let his assistant pastor handle the baptisms, marriage ceremonies, and such, while he and Catherine waited for news that Thomas Langley had been found drowned in the YMCA pool—a sad victim of the evils of alcohol. Only, no word ever came. No one found Thomas Langley's body. How was that possible?

Two days after the good Reverend Smith killed Langley, the phone calls started. At home, when Smith picked up the receiver, there was no one there—just heavy breathing, like someone gasping for air. Calls came to the church too, with the same eerie breathing. Then came the incident when Edward walked outside to his car and found a YMCA flyer tucked under the wiper blade. On a trip to the grocery store, he returned to find more YMCA flyers littered across his windshield.

When he got home from the store, Edward was hysterical for hours until Catherine finally convinced him that all these things were just coincidences—and that if he didn't get out of the house, he'd go insane. "Come with me to the movies, Ed," Catherine begged.

But the events at the movie theater were even more terrifying than anything Edward Smith had imagined. While he waited in line at the concession stand for popcorn, a young woman behind the counter handed him a T-shirt along with his order. He didn't have to look to know it was from the YMCA.

"Who told you to do this?" Smith demanded, his voice sharp.

The young woman looked startled. She pointed to the men's room door nearby. "He was there a second ago. I saw him when you walked up. The man told me to give this to you. He said it was a joke."

"What did he look like?"

She swallowed, clearly shaken. "He was tall. Thin. Kind of nice-looking. But... there was something strange about him. He looked wet."

Smith snatched the popcorn from the counter, threw down a dollar, and bolted for the theater. When he reached his seat and went to sit, he almost screamed. The cushion and even the backrest were soaked. "What is this, Catherine? Did you spill something?"

"Don't be silly, Ed. I didn't spill anything. I was in the ladies' room while you were in line. But I…"

Smith threw the box of popcorn at his wife and ran from the theater. He didn't look back, sprinting through the streets until he collapsed breathless on the curb. That's when he heard it: a voice—Thomas Langley's voice—whispering his name.

Smith didn't stick around to find out if it was God, a ghost, or his own madness. He ran the final blocks home and collapsed inside, where Catherine later found him curled on the floor, moaning. At the hospital, doctors warned he needed rest and no stress—his heart couldn't take it. They went home and waited. Waited for something. But a week passed, and still there was no word that Thomas Langley's body had been found.

A few nights later, things had quieted. Maybe it had all been coincidence. Or maybe he really was going insane. Then, one night…The house went dark. The rooms were cloaked in shadows. Catherine was visiting a sick parishioner, so it was up to Edward to fix the problem. He found the flashlight in the kitchen cabinet, but the batteries were weak. The stream of light barely reached a few feet in front of him—just enough to see the hallway and the door to the fuse box. But what the reverend wasn't expecting was what he saw along the way.

There, in the beam of the flashlight, wet footprints trailing across the floor. Water pooled around each step. Edward froze. His heart thundered in his chest. He followed the footprints, stopping when they ended in front of the hall coat closet. Slowly, he reached for the handle. His eyes adjusted to the dim light inside. Someone was there. *Thomas Langley.* He was drenched—his thick hair matted, his clothes clinging to his body, as if he had dragged the YMCA pool water with him.

"Hello, Edward," Langley said, calm and clear.

Smith opened his mouth, but no sound came. The flashlight slipped from his hand. He clutched his chest. The heart attack wasn't gradual this time; it hit like lightning. He knew it was happening. He could feel it, and he knew the Lord was taking him home. His knees gave way. His body collapsed, the breath knocked clean from his lungs.

* * *

Thomas Langley had almost drowned in the YMCA pool. When the Smiths dumped him in the water, he floated face-down until they left. He waited in the cold darkness until the sound of footsteps faded. Then he pulled himself from the pool, stumbled to his car, and drove—dripping wet—to the nearby hotel where he'd hidden a key under the front seat.

There, he showered, changed, and laid on the bed to plan. He wouldn't go home. Not yet. Edward might come looking for him. But in a few days, when the fear settled, Langley would begin: the phone calls, the flyers, the theater prank. All of it was to lead up to this one moment...the moment he stepped out of the coat closet.

* * *

There was a face looming over Edward Smith, peering down as if to judge whether he was dead. It wasn't Langley's face.

"Good job," the newcomer said. "Just the right amount of bang."

As if on cue, Thomas Langley leaned over and looked directly into Smith's dying eyes. "Are you sure this is going to kill him?" Langley asked. "We almost blew it, you know. You nearly got caught dumping water on the theater seat. But you've got to admit, *that* was the cherry on the cake."

He reached down and checked for a pulse. The reverend's hand dropped limply to the floor.

"And don't forget my cut," Langley said. "I need the money tomorrow. I'm leaving town until this all blows over. You can cover for me at the funeral. Not like anyone's missed me—they all think I'm traveling. You and Harold Raymond can enjoy your share of the do-re-mi. Though I don't know what you see in that guy... except for the boatload of money you had him steal."

"It wasn't from the collection plates. It was from the church account."

Langley laughed. "Yeah? Where do you think that money came from? It didn't fall from Heaven. Don't you know anything about church business?"

"Nothing. I never cared."

"Whatever," Langley said, reaching again for Smith's wrist. The pulse was faint. He stared, murderous and cold. "I can't believe Edward thought there was something between us. What a fool. After all this time, he didn't even know you. You have to admit, it was a good plan."

"Yes," Catherine Smith said, smiling. "It was a good plan, Thomas. Edgar Allan Poe would be proud."

THE HIGH SOCIETY DETECTIVE SERIES

The guest list is exclusive.
The alibis are charming.
The crimes are anything but accidental.

The High Society Detective Series follows a suave, sharp-eyed sleuth through the dark undercurrent of New York's elite— where everyone has something to lose and someone to hide.

ENJOY THE FULL SERIES...

- *The Fourteenth Man at Dinner*
- *Wine, Cheese, and Daggers (Are Back in Style)*
- *The Case of the Wrong Word*

* * *

MORE TITLES COMING SOON
Stay one step ahead of the next crime.

Visit the Amazon Author Page for new releases and updates:

www.amazon.com/author/marilynsporter

ABOUT THE AUTHOR

Marilyn Smith Porter is an American author known for her compelling mystery, suspense, and contemporary fiction. Her novels—including *The High Society Detective Series*, *Last Kiss*, and *Once More*—combine gripping plots with emotional depth and richly drawn characters. Marilyn's stories are filled with intrigue, romance, and unexpected twists that keep readers turning pages late into the night. With a talent for uncovering the extraordinary in everyday moments, she weaves secrets and heart into every story she tells. When she's not writing, Marilyn enjoys traveling, studying history, and discovering the hidden stories woven into real life.

www.ingramcontent.com/pod-product-compliance
Lightning Source LLC
Chambersburg PA
CBHW061919130726
47908CB00017B/2470